Mirvana

Mirvana
The story of my defiant love

Authored by

APOORVA

Disclaimer

This book has been published with all reasonable efforts taken to make the material error-free after the consent of the author. This book is sold subject to the condition that it shall not, by way of trade or otherwise, be lent, resold, or otherwise circulated without the copyright owner's prior written consent in any form of binding or cover other than that in which it is published and without a similar condition including this condition being imposed on the subsequent purchaser and without limiting the rights under copyright reserved above, no part of this publication maybe reproduced, stored in or introduced into a retrieval system or transmitted in any form or by any other means without the permission of the copyright owner.

Registered Office- 907-Sneh Nagar, Sapna Sangeeta Road, Agrasen Square, Indore – 452001 (M.P.), India
Website: http://www.wingspublication.com
Email: mybook@wingspublication.com

First Published by WINGS PUBLICATION 2020

Copyright © APOORVA 2020

Title: MIRVANA

Price: ₹ 299/- / $ 10

All Rights Reserved.

ISBN 978-81-946534-2-4

LIMITS OF LIABILITY/DISCLAIMER OF WARRANTY

Contents

CHAPTER
One

The Prologue

"Often what we feel like the end of the world is really a pathway to far better place".

— Karen Salmansohn

A similar situation came my way, a few months ago where, I found myself at the dead end of a yearlong journey of love.

I felt the pain in my heart; because nothing breaks like a heart. I said to myself, ***"Life is over, what you are going to do without your love around you"***. I had been so engrossed in this journey, so immersed into this feeling that I forgot it's just a chapter of life. But, ***"To let go was really difficult"***.

I took a day off to solitude and went to one of my favorite places, a very beautiful resort, of a very dear friend.

Those few hours in the lap of nature, among chirping birds and fresh Breeze rejuvenated my soul, heart and mind. The sunset was beautiful. So many wandering thoughts came to a standstill. I could actually concentrate on the center of bright red dawning Sun for a few moments.

My soul meditated to the tunes of the universal phenomenon of sunset. My whole existence which was gasping for a breath of fresh air for last one year, calmed down. I heard a very deep and intense echo of my soul. It was telling me to relive.

I said to myself, *"It's just the beginning, look at the brighter side, in last one year you have grown on the path of love, you have changed to a better person, you have touched hearts and souls of people around you, your attitude has melted someone's heart towards betterment, how can you purge for little un-fulfillments when you have gained so many precious fulfilments in many ways.*

Let the world know your growth as a reward of journey and not as the failure of un-fulfillment". That was it...

Though, I am not from literature background but I decided to jot down those few turning points, which were milestone of my growth in last one year. I decided to name this humble piece of writing as **MIRVANA**. The best suited meaning of *Mirvana*, as I checked on our dear Google was *"Life lessons and challenges"*. It says, "Key lessons we should be learning in life, is about understanding; that even negative memories have a role. At the same time; life challenge is linked to battling any thoughts which compels us to think that the situations for us are not good enough".

Thank you,

Dipti and Rohit for being a part of my life
and medium of this inspiration.

CHAPTER

Two

The Zing

Why, when, how, what and where are the main questions which befit in all situations of our lives, at all ages and all stages. I was three when the question came to my mind, when I had a sibling to share my parents love, at five when I had to go to school, at ten to score well in my exams, at fifteen when I had to leave school and move to college, at nineteen when college was over and I had to look for a job and also suitors for my marriage, at 20 when I got a job and had to leave home, at 21 when I got a marriage proposal, at 22 when I got married, at 24 when I had to choose between 'stagnation in a relation' or 'my peace of mind', and now when I was at 34, I encountered a situation, where the dust of resentment of past relationship which was clogged over last ten years on my heart, suddenly got blown away.

It was that masculine groovy voice on phone that blew away the dust of ten years and entered straight into the core of my heart. My heart "Zinged" for him at that very moment. I was so mesmerized that my mind strayed off to a different world. I don't remember what we spoke, all I remember till this moment is the warmth and intensity of that voice.

I don't remember any man in last ten years, who could leave such a deep impact on me in our first conversation ever. There was definitely something which pulled my stings.

After the phone call, when I returned to my normal self, I silenced my racing heart, **"At his age he must be father of two kids, so shut up and get to work, this happens only in fairy tales…The Zing"**.

I had no other option but to listen to my brain. I packed up my bags and shifted to new city, among new people, new set of colleagues including him. The work place was full of happy faces, warm environment, accommodating set of people and a wonderful team.

On day one, in the new city, I got an invitation for dinner and my ZING got the responsibility to take me along. I saw him for the first time, in very dim light at the porch…he was sitting in his car. His face was bright and shining, I could not even have a full glance. In five minutes journey to our destination, I could feel a unique obscure silence in the car. There was no conversation except for an evening greeting. We both were silent in the car enjoying that obscure vacuum of silence.

At the dinner, I came to know…'he was single'… **_What??? Is It???_**….The answers to why, what, why, how and where, about my sudden relocation to that place were amply clear to me now.

On the way back, the vacuum had doubled than before. We both were equally conscious. The journey of five min was like hours long. We dint know each other, we dint know what to say, we dint even know how to behave with each other at that moment. Even '*GOOD NIGHT*' was very sober.

Although, I was in a relationship before but had never sensed this kind of emotion ever in my bones. I was thinking to myself on the way back to my room, "*You are 34 and he is 38, but you both are behaving like teenagers. Does tender love still exists in this tinder age? Is it love blooming?*" **Oh...shut up girl....not again!!!**

Believe me...that was one beautiful night. I was, what I was again. The empress inside me was reborn. I felt like a woman again. I felt, being me again. I could feel the abundant love in my heart again. I felt, I am living and breathing again. All this was happening when ZING had just happened.

I thanked god before sleeping, as he had chosen me for this feeling. I was confident that everything was a larger planning to bring both of us around. Everything happens for a reason and I knew the reason now. I slept smilingly with my heart full of love and hope.

THE ZING WAS WORKING...

CHAPTER
Three

The Teenage was Back

Am I a 34 years old woman or 16 years young girl? The days subsequent to the zing were just like in a fairy tale. The surroundings were beaming with love; Was it their essence or my reflection in them?

I felt like stocking up my dressing table again. Changed my wardrobe completely. The shades of lip colors and the fragrance of the perfumes were my new interest. My orthodox way of living to avoid an eye on me took a U-turn, now I wanted someone to notice me. I never dared to experiment with my hair, but now I was all set to groom them with fringes.

I had never graduated from a bun, but now loose hair were my new way of styling without apprehensions. I would wear my saari with all tucks and pins, but now I could flaunt the attire. Not to forget the most beautiful ornament a woman can wear *"The smile"* which I wore in my eyes more than on my lips.

> *Oh God!! Am I awake or in a dream?*
> *Is it me or someone else inside me?*

I suddenly felt that I had started to love myself in order to love him. Our teacher often used to tell us *"Self Love is most important, because we can only give what we have. We can't love someone if we don't love ourselves"*. I always wandered on this logic.

The reason was, my understanding or I would admit misunderstanding of the depth of this statement. I used to feel, *"Isn't it being selfish, if Self Love is priority over love for other?"* But now the meaning was clear to me. I had understood, that I can fill others cup of love if my own cup is full and overflowing.

After years of battle within myself, with many not so good situations and not so good surrounding in my life, I could find my real self-back. My heart was always chirping within, my eyes had their glitter back, my fingers would move like a magician's fingers and had started talking as if they had voice, my vocal cords had sweetened *(though I have a manufacturing fault of loud voice)*. My sense of humor was improving day by day, my efficiency in work had increased *(so I get time to spend with my love)*, songs started to play in my ears all the time, my pores were happy. I could feel his love in my skin and bones. I was blushing and beaming due to one small feeling which was yet one sided.

This tiny but powerful feeling had changed me completely in no time. I would admit, I had changed and had changed for good. I hadn't felt as good in years about myself. I felt, I was alive again and was ready to walk on the unknown roads without any map. I had gathered my courage back, so I can experiment in my life.

I felt, I was "*Alice in wonderland*" and will write my own story my way. I was confident about this fateful meeting. I was sure it's conspired by the universe for two of us. I was glowing brighter with every passing day.

Was it love for him or I was happy to rediscover myself due to love for him? Whatever it was... I was enjoying every bit of it. I just wanted to live in this moment and nowhere else.

*My teenage was back and my love was nothing less than an Elixir or a Philosopher stone...
as it had suddenly made me precious...*

CHAPTER
Four

Heart Vs Mind

I was yet enjoying the bliss of my newly found love, which was blossoming with every moment within my heart. Suddenly my mind sounded a bell in my head…*"Sorry for interruption, it's a wakeup call from your mind… hello…is it love or infatuation? Please clarify before you get trapped"..*

Oh my God! How could I be so careless about it? The mind is right it can be an infatuation…what's the future of this feeling….is it really love? In a few moments many questions crossed by my mind…How will I find out?

Now this is what you call a nightmare. My heart dint want to part with the feeling, but the mind was trying to pull me back as it could be a trap. Can I afford to get into a heart break or a stagnant situation again?

That day, I realised how difficult it is to bring heart and mind on a common table for discussion. Those few days were very difficult to calm, the battle of heart and mind down and listen to the voice of my soul. It was during that time, when I could decipher that heart and mind are equally talkative, argumentative, illogical, bossy, tantrum kings and "Mr. I know everything".

The battle was between heart for love and mind for infatuation and both were not bringing a common point for a resolution. Even my meditations failed. Now what was the way out? My love was about to go on a month long break. I hardly had any time left to let him know about my feelings. The battle was yet unresolved and on top of that the fear had sunk in. What a MESS I was.

One fine day, I sat in the garden, it was a pleasant outside. The breeze was flowing through my hair and was touching my skin. It had such a cooling effect on my heart and mind that I got a widow of silence. I closed my eyes and felt that silence to the core of my soul. It was so calming that my eyes started to flow. These tears were sign of deep healing my soul was experiencing at that time. I let that moment live within me for two hours. I didn't move, I didn't control my tears, I didn't say anything. I felt grounded and my soul started to answer.

The soul said, "***Why are you doubting your intuition? Its powerful, its blessed, its fearless, its confident, its wise, its keen to learn, it wants to be courageous…Give it a chance to grow. Growth is not about success, it's about learning lessons…Let it explore…let it learn…let it grow…Trust yourself more than anything***". I suddenly realised I was not alone in the garden, there were people around. I went back to my room.

Whom was I talking to? Was it God or my soul? I had never heard any of these two, talking so loudly and clearly with me. Now this was something I dint know how to deal with, but I believe in source and energy so I told myself to rewind the conversation in my mind. I repeatedly rewound the same statement till I understood it completely.

All I could understand was to believe in my intuition and take a leap of faith, in order to learn new lesson and grow beyond, what I was at the moment. Now I was clear as to what it was. ***A deep lesson of life comes from a deep emotional construction or destruction. The deep emotion is love which gives courage to have faith and take a chance.***

I was feeling powerful, contented and so full of emotional balance. It was only love and nothing else, but a situation was waiting to testify the same. I remembered a quote by "**Lao Tzu**"

> *"Mastering others is strength,*
> *Mastering yourself is true power".*

CHAPTER
Five

The Transformation

The transformation is a big term. Small changes collectively cause transformation and transformation as a whole may be termed as growth. We grow only if we are ready to change or bring the change or be a part of the change.

I was preparing for a lecture in which I had to explain "The Fibonacci Principle". As I Googled it, various links opened. I checked almost every links and in one of them an analogy was drawn for life. As per the logic of that principle, a person undergoes changes at the age of 0, 1,1,2,3,5,8,13,21,34,555,89. Today I was recollecting every bit I could, from my childhood till date. I was 34 and as per the sequence it was definitely the stipulated age for change.

"Does it refer to small changes?"

"No, it does not". It is that big transformation, which occurs after numerous small changes

"Yes, that's right, if I only analyse the time between 21 years and 34 years, I have undergone a complete "SINE

CURVE" through all rises and falls in my personal and professional life. Here I stand today, as a completely transformed woman, much better version of what I was at 21 years of age, a much grown up woman intellectually, a much confident person as a whole. I believe, a new chapter is about to begin with new people, new agendas of life, new experiences, new learning and another new me".

Off late, I had many vivid dreams of various people and places. Somehow I remember them very clearly. I saw visions, even when I was wide awake. All these coincidences were coming out to be true. So, I spoke to one of the acquaintance, who had spiritual inclination and she told me that those were the symptoms of the spiritual awakening.

It was a fact, that right from my childhood, I was drawn to the ghost stories, fairy tales, mythology and magic, Metaphysics, Divinations and was always curiosity to know the abstract. **"Who am I? What is the purpose of my life?"** I got an opportunity to know the answers to my questions and I grabbed the opportunity.

Many things were happening simultaneously in my life, in a very short span of time. It was, as if the fruit of struggle of last 12 years is now being bestowed by the divine.

It was this day, when I correlated the experience of grounding, which I had a few days ago, when my heart and mind were not looking eye to eye. Yes it was that day, when I actually connected to my soul.

The most powerful emotion of love, which I was refraining for years had hit me like a storm and had changed my life. The moment I accepted love, it triggered the spiritual awakening.

In that one month, I had achieved patience. My horizons had widened. I was no more a slave to my mind, thoughts and judgments. The changes were taking place for years, but I had probably accepted it now. I was loving that **"New Me"** and was ready to discover more. I was grounded, humble, connected to the source and a being of love.

The thought itself was so mesmerizing that
I was eager to experience it and live it.

CHAPTER
Six

The First Reflection

I was discovering myself every day. The calmness which I was trying to achieve for years had suddenly fructified. I was much at peace in spite of the overflow of unexpressed feeling of love to my love.

The environment was acting as a catalyst to let this chemical reaction succeed at a faster pace. The teasing and taunting to both the singles was at it's peak.

We both became conscious, we would not make an eye contact, we would stand in different groups, we would have our tea separately, avoid talking and what not? I used to smile within and laugh at the plight of both of us.

We both were behind schedule for love, almost 20 years and 18 years. What should have happened to us in 18 and 16 years of age was happening at 38 and 34. **Love is ageless, it's timeless**.

Till now everything was happening accept the expression of the feelings. *How to tell it to him that I had feelings for him? Will I have enough courage? Will I be able to speak? When would I do it? Will it be right to tell him? How will he react? Will it spoil our professional understanding? Shall I even compare this feeling with profession? Is it unethical? What if he already has someone on his mind?*

The contemplation went on in my mind for many days. In the middle of this dilemma, one fine day I had a very beautiful premonition. What I saw in a few seconds is as fresh as its happening in front of my eyes right now. *I saw, I was sitting at study, writing something. He came with two cups of coffee, while placing a cup on my table he said, "This new place and new set of people will be really tiring". I looked at him smiled and said, "I am sure you will handle it well, it was your heartiest desire to achieve this status".* We both smiled looking into each other's eyes and the vision got over.

It was not even a month that I had met him, but the emotions for him were so intense that firstly I had a vision about him, secondly what was this vision about and thirdly how do I know his heartiest desires? It was a big reflection of my feelings for him.

I had no idea about how much of this will be true? Whole night I was thinking about this vision, tried every permutation and combination to decode it.

After hours of contemplation I came on the conclusion that firstly he will have a change of place, secondly he will get promoted, thirdly we both will be confidants of each other one day to share our worries and happiness. I decided to tell him about the vision but only first two points not the third one.

The night took extra hours to pass. I was waiting for the morning eagerly. I got ready an hour before the office time. I reached office early, finished my morning rush and started to wait for him.

He reached but I could not gather courage to go to his office. I had not been to his office ever since I had been at that place. **How will I begin with this topic?** A person having premonition for another person who is just an acquaintance was not normal, more abnormal was this concept. Everyone does not believe in such concepts.

The clock was showing '1' PM. I gathered courage and walked up to his office, he was alone. I wished him '**Good afternoon sir**'. He replied with his charming smile. He asked me for coffee, I said, "Sure sir, thank you". Now I had time.

There was long silence as both of us were unable to speak to each other. I sipped some water and asked him in very feeble voice, "Is there any good restaurant around sir"? He smiled and started telling me about places. All I could feel was his voice touching my ears. *I wish, he could feel that too. I wish he could continue speaking. "The most soothing voice is the voice of the person you love".*

The peon got the coffee and conversation stopped. While sipping my coffee I asked him, "*Sir, may I say something?*" He looked at me with doubtful eyes as if he was suspecting that I was going to say, "I love you". With a little question mark in his voice he said, "*Oh...h...k*" tell me? He looked straight into my eyes and waited for me to speak.

I gulped a big sip of coffee out of fear, took a deep breath and in fast forward said, "*Sir, yesterday I had a premonition about you*". *He asked, "What's premonition"?* I explained to him, what premonition means. He smiled and moved his head in doubtful agreement to the concept.

Anyways... I continued and told him everything. He thought for a while, smiled and said, "I don't have necessary qualification for this promotion, so there is no chance of promotion". I smiled, but with more confidence this time and asked him, when will the promotion list be out? He said, "Anytime now, but I am not hopeful". I said, ***"We shall see who wins; my belief or your calculations?"***

I got up from his office and came back smiling. The fear of striking a conversation had vanished. Finally after almost a month, the ice between both of us broke.

I was happy, because first reflection about him was positive, good and expressive and I could share it with him. The biggest thing was that he listened to it and aired his opinion in the outcome, in spite of his disbelief.

It was difficult to speak and more difficult was to speak about Psychic ability to a person who doesn't believe in Metaphysics, Theosophy and concept of source energy. The first conversation and ice breaking was on the most difficult topic.

Now onwards things will be easier. I was happy that I could be transparent to him without any fear of being judged. I dint know anything about him, all I knew was that I loved him. I was off guard and vulnerable in front of him but I was not afraid. I think my vulnerability for him was my strength. I loved this side of mine.

I had seized my moment...

CHAPTER
Seven

The Decision day

I was kind of relieved after ice breaking in conversing with my love. It was 40th day in new place, among new people including my love. I got a news in the morning that he was leaving for a month.

"Oh Hell…I haven't told anything to him. He will leave? How will I manage? I will miss him. He is going for a month; what if he comes back engaged? What if he meets someone new who is more charming?"

I was worried …Was it actually a worry or fear of losing him? Isn't it strange, how a completely unknown person creates an apartment in your heart and your happiness gets so dependent on that one unknown person?

Till now, I dint know anything about him or his feelings. But, that day was a situation of '*Do or Die*'. I decided to take a leap of faith and express my feelings to him… *But how?*

By the time I figured out *"How?"* it was past office time. I returned home, I was not hungry at all. I just picked up my pen and started writing. The feelings were too many and words were too less. I had a lot to tell but could not find the right words for my sesquipedalian. I drafted, redrafted and re-re-drafted and what came out in the end was:

Dear Sir,

Today, I have picked up my pen and I don't know what I would scribble on the paper. But, I don't wish to miss this moment, when I have gathered courage to express, I can't miss this chance. The situation may be completely different once you are back. I may not be in similar frame of mind and tangled with other issues of my life. I might have had reconciled with the status quo or would have changed my mind, due to fear of failure, so on and so forth.

I am writing this letter, under the influence of the woman inside me to the man inside you. Only that man can understand, who has left a little scope for him to listen to the woman. Please take a deep breath and bear with me once. The contents are very simple, no riddles, no phrases.

After completing 30 years of age, a woman has nothing to lose except her self-respect and character. I have put both at stake while picking up this pen today. But somewhere deep inside my heart, I trust you. I don't know the reason, but I always find myself off guard and vulnerable in front of you. In spite of feeling insecure, I feel good. Even the best or worst of your comments are soothing to my ears. I never knew, what it was like, to look at someone and smile for no reason.

I know, I am already minus one while I am writing all this to you. All I can say in my justification is that; I had to close those doors, because they were not leading me anywhere else, except death. I chose to live and chose to experience all those feelings which had remained unfulfilled, deep inside my heart. I was reborn on 12th may 2009 that's why my heart is like in teens. Life has given me enough training to be brave and strong though.

I want to write everything which is there inside me right now, but I will leave it unspoken. Over flow of emotions may not be good for me. I believe if the man has understood and felt the essence of the words of this letter, he will be able to decipher what has been left unspoken. That's all from a woman to a man.

Sir, if you feel I have crossed my limits, please forgive me. You have already learnt the art of surviving alone but I am still trying to learn it. I think life is too short to hide your feelings and have vengeance against the person who has already surrendered. Please don't mistake this with the word desperation because, though it would be difficult, but I can still accept a 'NO' gracefully and also, your scolding.

Warm Regards

We both were staying next door, so I decided to handover this letter to him, just before going to the party. I got ready and kept the letter inside my pocket. The moment I entered the venue, a few colleagues had already come. One of them gave the news, "**Sir got promoted**". It was '**The News**' to my ears.

I got flooded with mixed emotions. I was '**Happy-Sad**'. Happy for the progress of my love and sad because I had decided, not to give that letter to him. I thought, it might trigger him, let him handle one surprise at a time. There was a crowd of known faces, but all I could see was his face glowing with happiness and eyes shining with pride. I felt contented to see that happiness on his face. I observed that 70mm smile for the first time ever since I know him. I really felt his happiness in the depth of my heart. This strange emotion filled me up to the brim.

The party got over and we shook hands. As far as I remember that was the only time we shook hands till date. I returned to my room and my eyes were full of tears. *Is this how it feels like, to live through the happiness of the one you love?*

It was, as if it's my personal achievement. My heart was living in this moment as its own as a right. I thanked god for his blessings. Whatever I had seen in the reflection, a few days ago had materialized to the reality.

The day did not end in a way I had thought it would, but in a way that it was destined. It ended as the D-Day of my love's wish fulfillment in profession instead of the day of wish fulfillment of my love for '*My Love*'. I think, if it had to be his wish versus my wish, it has ended in the best possible manner.

The saying is so true, **"Man proposes, God disposes".** Though the D-Day did not end as I had intended it to, but finally I was happy and contented.

My D-Day was yet awaited...

CHAPTER
Eight

The Resolve

The minimum journey to D-Day was 30 days. I could not sleep that night. We both were just Next Door to each other; *so near but so far.* We were breathing in the same air. We will breathe in the same air again, after 30 days now.

Though, I was familiar to this sadness, still it took time for me to bear it. I couldn't sleep for a minute that night. *What had happened to me? Why this one person mattered so much to me that I had to think for an outlet for next 30 days.*

I remembered, I used to scribble down my feelings in my school and college days. I was famous for my few good pieces of writing. I remembered, that I was blessed with the power of expression, without uttering a word. No one other than my pen could be my best friend.

While I was making this plan of writing I realised, it was ever since 2006 that I had written anything. It's a gap of 12 years, am I still left with some talent? A second thought of how I had stopped writing, haunted me to my core. It was a man, whose betrayal had damaged me to the extent of a virtual death and rebirth. I had died many times and was reborn many times, in last 12 years.

The survival consumed my complete energy. I was left with nothing more than surviving to invest in my growth. Today, it's a man again whose sheer presence around has triggered the feeling in the form of self-love inside me. I am talking about my growth today. I am reconnecting with my own qualities and talent again. **Why not? Why shall I not do it?**

I will tap this journey to D-Day, as an opportunity to think ahead of Survival and progress towards growth. Let me check my own waters. So, I decided to write everything I feel every day, in the form of a letter to my love.

I was sure enough, it's going to be tough but was equally sure that it will lead me to beautiful path of self-awareness. I did not know what would be the content but I definitely knew, it would be pure feelings, complete truth and fearless expression.

That day, I was no more afraid of being judged. See, I was growing step-by-step and was overcoming my fears one by one. I had no idea, how this decision of mine, will affect me? I was just sure enough that I was going to stick to this resolve, '*come what may*'.

At the end of that night, I was wandering, how uncertain the life of a person can be…The situations can turn tables anytime. A situation which was once a reason of turning my life upside down, was now the reason of my happiness and self-realization. I was all determined to befriend my fountain pen again.

Mr. Parker let's see how long can we scroll together…

CHAPTER
Nine

Day-One

Day one at office, without him was not good. I was physically there but mentally with my love. My colleagues tried to find that casual smile on my face but got nothing. ***Missing someone and not being able to see him is the worst feeling ever.***

I wish, I could tell him, those little moments spent with him in the office, mattered so much. I was sad and anxious. I was missing him terribly. In fact, I used to miss him even when he was around. This feeling was familiar to me, ***but why with him***?

Missing someone, feeling lonely and similar situations from old chapters of life, coming out simultaneously, were making me feel under confident and vulnerable. I had not spoken about that episode even to my own self as much in detail in last 10 years. I went into the flashback and my pen started enumerating the same situation of incompleteness and life coming to a standstill.

Dear Sir,

Day one at office, without you being around, was not so good. My feet didn't move to the next door. I have never felt so restless in last 8 years, ever since I overcame my past injuries.

Indeed, it's not an unfamiliar feeling, but definitely it is unpleasant. I underwent this suffocation, anxiety and restlessness, when I was trying to explore every possible method to save my marriage, but the man walked away leaving me in the middle of nowhere, without a closure.

All I could see was darkness, sealed windows and closed doors. Six days in that confinement were like a dead end. I was completely blank, didn't know, whom to call for help? My brain was numb and heart was broken. After six days I realised, I was alive. I repeated it to myself "you are not dead". **For sure what doesn't kill you makes you stronger.**

But why am I writing all this to you?

Sorry, I got emotional. Today, I am not even sure if these letters would ever reach their destination? I am surprised on myself, I never opened the doors of my heart for anyone after the betrayal. You just gate crashed, without any early warning and melted my heart effortlessly.

I am writing all this in the condition of my heart in molten state. You may come back engaged, commited or married, what will I do? How will I behave? I have not thought about that. **I love you is a truth, you love me back is not yet a truth.**

I will not force myself upon you for sure. I am mature enough to understand what love is like, at the same time, I assume you too are mature enough to understand, that anyone can fall in love with anyone, at any point and time.

Emotions are free rebels and they don't listen to mind. I had to rein in these rebels yesterday. I wanted to steal you from everyone in the party for a moment, hug you tight and say "**Congratulations**".

I wish, I could tell you that my love for you is unconditional. I don't expect or demand anything from you. I have loved you the way you are, irrespective of your place in profession. If at all, we get a chance to spend this life together, I will not steal your dear Saturdays, I will not demand anything except some space in your heart.

I know I am **XL** size, at the same time I am aware that my heart has led me to you because the size of your heart is **XXL**.

We are different, but in a way, we are the same. You are Lacoste; I am Global Desi. You love coffee; I love tea, you like solitude; I am a social animal, you speak less; I am a Chatterbox. We complement each other. Life is all about adventures and being on a roller coaster of thrills. I am feeling so much better.

See, how important it is to communicate. I just imagined you, sitting in front of me with your active mind, naughty smile and listening to me; waiting for "**kidding**" on some point in the conversation.

Believe me, I am not pricking anything with a hope that something will fall on my table (as you muttered yesterday). I am being truthful *and straight forward, I think you will respect this feeling. Accepting or not is completely your choice.*

LOTS OF LOVE...

I was much in my peaceful state of mind. I really felt he was listening to all this sitting in front of me. I was wondering within myself, **"In this tinder age, is it wise to have a Tender Heart"?**

I will wait for the answer...

CHAPTER
Ten

Small Gestures

Second day, his favorite day; Saturday, passed very quickly in office. I didn't feel like going anywhere could not even concentrate on my prayers. I felt a part inside me was missing.

I sat down with a cup of coffee (not the tea) and started thinking. I need to pour out this emptiness, but to my surprise, *my agony aunt* was not there, nor was he bothered to respond to "*Good afternoon sir*". All I could receive as a reply was, "yes indeed". ***What?... Does he know what I feel?*** The reply to **Good afternoon sir**...was as if he is poking me towards more sadness intentionally. I felt ignored and unwanted.

What shall I discuss with him today? I was sad and angry at the same time. I thought about last 40 days and the incidents between me and him. "***Oh my God... what an ignorant I am? The catalyst were working both ways, he is mature enough to sense the Vibe. I could never avoid blushing and sobering down in front of him. That means, he knows my feelings for him***".

Sadness suddenly vanished and I started smiling. Such a relief it was. I thought, it would be easier to express. The next moment I was angry.

"If he knows... why doesn't he tell me?"

But why should he tell you... he might be testing your waters. He might be waiting for you to speak out.

"Then why is he poking me to add to my sadness"?

Stupid girl he is enjoying the attention.

"Oh come on... he is a charmer, he must not be lacking attention anyways. I am sure girls must have given him enough attention in last 20 years that he never felt the need of companionship. He may not even understand the essence of my love"

How do you say he is a charmer?

A man who could gate crash my heart has to be a charmer. If I analyse critically about the fact "Who can be my man?" he may not fit into the criteria.

I am outgoing, he is introvert; in longer run, this quality may over shadow him. He doesn't make eye contact with anyone; this may be due to lack of self-confidence, more so it's not acceptable in a man who has worked in this profession for 17 years now. This drawback will not allow him to accept me the way I am, because we are working for same organization and comparison are very common practice here.

He does not speak out which is an indication of deep wounds or deep secrets. I can heal him with my love, but is he ready to accept this help? The answer is 'NO', because of his false self-preservation technique, **"Neither shall I speak, nor would someone know".**

How do you say all this, you haven't even spoken to him as much?

I am a woman and I am born with a Sixth Sense, moreover God has gifted me with good intuition, I can see through a person. I agree in his case I am biased due to my love for him and I discount many qualities which are not acceptable in a man. When you love someone the information just flows in.

Then why do you love him?

I can't answer why, but I can answer how I love him.

I love him unconditionally, I love his negative traits, trust him without any fear, I can be myself with him without apprehension of being judged. He is not my need, he is my desire. I feel his happiness as mine, I pray for him every day, I connect with his soul telepathically. I cannot see him in pain. I don't want anything from him. I pick up his energies as mine. I can read his eyes, irrespective of the deception and facade he puts on. Even if he says a **NO** *I think, I will still live with a hope that every day is a new day and the change is only constant in life.*

After this internal cross examination session; I sipped my coffee and began my letter:

Dear Sir,

You are aware that I am sad. You have taken a part of me with you. Small gestures of replying to one odd message on phone may relieve me of my agony for some time. **'Yes indeed'** *triggered me to an internal cross examination session today.*

It's a fact that in last 40 days, I have seen you as a colleague, I am yet to interact with the man inside you. This is also a fact that you have also seen me as your colleagues, you are yet to know the woman inside me. Today I have decided to introduce this woman to the man she desire for.

She was born to a very simple couple and a very humble family of Himachal Pradesh. Due to her father's job, she was brought up in a small town of Punjab. She was not born with a silver spoon but was born with a silver heart.

She was fortunate to get love from two couples, her biological parents and you can say, her Foster parents. Foster parents were a Sikh couple, they didn't have any biological heir. Their adopted son expired at 24 in a road accident. As our neighbor, they found some solace in the giggles of this small girl.

The love and bonding between both the families strengthened and the families were ever inseparable. A girl born to a Hindu family, given a Christian name and brought up in Sikh environment, a complete secular.

She got her first Suitor at the age of 16, the moment she cleared 12th. She was clear in her head that she has to have her own identity before marrying a man of her parents' choice. She asked for four years from her parents before considering marriage proposal for her. The wish was granted with a few condition; **No affairs, the respect of parents and family be maintained and timelines be followed strictly.**

She worked hard and achieved her wish well within the timeline. At the age a few months past 20 she had her own identity.

The first battle was over, but there were more challenges waiting on the new path. In the male dominated profession she was a lone worrier. With a few pluses and minuses she grew up with her team and her team grew up with her.

During initial six months she encountered episodes which enlightened her to be a "**Woman of Substance**". So she decided to be in her own '**Tigress skin**', "If people think I am arrogant; I will live up to it, but won't give up my self-respect at any cost".

At 22, a man walked up to her with a proposal, "**Sir if you are looking forward for an affair, I am not the one**". No it's more than that. "**In that case please approach my parents**". The marriage was solemnized, next 2 years were awful. She was manhandled, manipulated, emotionally tortured, dominated and when all this was not enough for her nervous breakdown she was subjected to graver agonies.

She survived all this because she was left with a few more years of life. Survived a physical death but could not help the death of her simplicity, her innocence, her trust, her love, her patience, her feeling and many emotions which can't be described in words. **'It was dark at the outside but darker inside of her'**. This was not the end, it was a beginning of another new chapter.

Most difficult battle is to fight your loved ones. So far the battle was between him and her, but now she had to ruffle feathers with him, his family, her family, society, professional rivals(who could not get a chance to roll over so far) and above all her own self.

She was broken, torn apart into pieces and scattered all over. It's blood curdling to explain the journey of revival. It gives me chills down my Spine and a shooting pain to the core of my soul. All I wish to mention here is that she is thankful to God to put her through this rigmarole and to give her strength to undergo the test.

She could know herself and her potential, it has made her a better person and a good human. She is much grounded and stable. She would have never realised her worth, if the man would not have betrayed her.

"Sometimes one has to get knocked down lower than one ever has been to stand up taller than one ever was". Today she is standing tall as a Victor not as a victim. Her biggest victory was the forgiveness to the sinner.

People played important role in her life. She can still categories them into two. The first are those who discount the others struggle due to immaturity and are still stuck to prove the unprovable. The second are those who have seen her through the struggle of losing herself and reviving again as a stronger one.

She has equal number of admirers and critics. People know her as **No-Nonsense Woman, Hell of a Women, Sweet, Devil and what not**? She is perfectly fine even if people talk behind her back. She believes in **Catching the Bull by Its Horns**. Men enough will always come in front and confront, cowards don't matter much. She feels, if people are talking she is worth their attention, she may be a threat to their existence due to her strong personality, so be it.

It's too much for many to handle irrespective of their gender. So, she is generally misunderstood. She lives with a few tags. Being straight forward is tagged as immaturity, being open to conversations over confrontations is being too much. Being happy and ever smiling (she hates being sad) is tagged as invitation. Expressive is tagged as available.

At any cost, she does not want shoulder of shallow people with vested interest, so she doesn't cry. She has learnt the art of crying inwards if need be. As a woman it's soothing to have a genuine person around to vent out. She is looking for a genuine person, who can dare to be with her, who can put a little effort to see through the hard shell and reach her softer core. Who can respect the struggle which has made her the way she is today, who can trust her.

In last 9 years, she has not come across any. Her softer side is a bonus to that man who can *accept this stronger side of hers. She cannot take chance by reversing the sequence of acceptance.*

*To conclude this letter I wish to tell you that so far many chapters have begun and ended. Here I have started a new chapter, **though my search has come to a halt but the reply is still in waiting.** I only know two things; **I love my love and I trust God and myself.***

Thank you for reading such a long letter and bearing with this disjointed piece of writing it made me feel good, so I did it.

Take Care... Come Back Soon...

Human emotions are so complex. One small lack of gesture at his end had triggered so much of turbulence inside of me that I ended up expressing so much. I believe one must not remember any sad and bad memories. One has lived with them once and one should not re-live them at any cost, but today reliving last 34 years was worth it.

I realised, irrespective of the bad patches here is a life I have lived so far, which I am proud of. yes that's true, I am proud of myself that I lived my life as a 'Woman of Worth', 'Wonder Woman' Who still believes in love, a woman who is not afraid to face her fears and above all I am the heroine of my own story.

I take responsibility to take my own decisions and live by them come what may.

CHAPTER
Eleven

The Faith

> ***"Faith is the Bird that feels the light when the dawn is still dark."***
>
> *— "Unknown"*

I think, it was my faith that made me feel that he knows, I am talking to him every day. I am discussing various matters of life and emotions with him. It was as if we both were sitting face to face and talking to each other. ***May be love is felt like this!***

Would he ever understand what these letters meant to our bonding? I decided not to create the mountain of doubt, when I can move them with my faith. With every passing day, I was being more open in discussing more difficult topics. I had no reason to justify why it was happening, but I was feeling like believing it.

It was just the third day he had left and I was overcoming my fears and progressing towards faith. I was willing to risk anything to God on this situation. I was able to concentrate on my prayers. What I saw as a very beautiful vision during my prayer strengthened my faith. That faith enabled me to communicate with my love telepathically and my love was making it easier to communicate with him. What emerged out on paper as communication was:

Dear Sir,

I must call you a 'BUGGER'. You just don't respond. I don't bombard you, with message that are difficult to answer. I know, I bug you with a 'Good Morning' or 'Good Afternoon' but that's not being too much...isn't it? With you, my maturity vanishes, I don't pretend to attract you, as I don't feel the need of it. This is the reflection of trust for you in my heart.

After introducing the woman to a man, I am feeling light. I am fine and happy today. I am feeling love in the air. The insecurity and fear of losing you to someone else are no longer there. I have left my love to faith. I have told God, **"I can't wait to see how you do it?"** I am sure my goddess will choose the best for me and my heart says you are the best for me. Ooh......did I say the best? Gosh...so absent minded, I meant '**the Beast**'.

I want to tell you that I am not a psychologist and I don't judge people. I definitely put in efforts to know people. I tried knowing you, but you just don't open up to the conversation.

I tried to peep into your soul. You would be surprised to know that your soul is much more expressive and communicative than you. How do I know? Wait... I shall explain...

I read the book 'The Secret' that gave me an insight to the universe and power of thoughts, the law of Attraction. I practice, what I learn. I have my own ways to decode the mysteries. I like to experiment with what I know, to explore what I don't know. So I used a little spiritual knowledge I have to know your spirit. I sat for my prayers, connected to your soul telepathically. Your soul responded to the invitation, the scenario unfolded like this:

"My soul, as a 10 years old girl, knocked at the doors of your room. Your soul, as a same aged boy opened the door. Both moved out to lawns. Both were holding hands and looking into each other's eyes very intensely. They played, watered plants and finally sat together.

My soul prompted yours, "Why are you so calm and sad?" In reply, your soul put its head in the lap of my soul and closed its eyes. It remained in that situation for 37 minutes. Then, your soul got up and said, "Finally someone knocked the door but you will have to give me time". I asked "How much time?" He said, "One month".

I am sharing all this with you because I want you to know everything about me. I am aware, all this may not synchronize with your logic, that's fine with me. My spiritual beliefs have never harmed anyone and I have a reason to believe in it, in the same manner you must be having reasons not to believe in it.

You are always in my prayers. The day you express your disbelief in getting a promotion, I had petitioned to the source energy, I worship. She accepted it, I cried out of happiness and gratitude to her. I know you won't ask anything for yourself from anyone, but someone had to pray for you.

Enough of spirituality for today. Let's go off to sleep now, I want to see you in my dreams.

GOOD NIGHT

I was realizing that love for him was much deeper than I thought it would be. I had not got attracted to him on physical plain or sexually. The connection was definitely on much at spiritual level, soul contract or an old bonding. He never said anything to me ever, still I always felt that he wanted to open up but something is stopping him.

Today when his soul healed in the lap of my soul for 37 minutes, I felt complete. We communicated so much in that silence. My whole focus shifted from '**what I feel for him**' to '**what he feels and why?**'

A little faith had pushed me to a new dimension of exploring the possibilities. I feel, it's not only love which has brought us together in this situation, but it's going to be much more. I was trying a method to connect with him, Telepathy has helped me and I am going to explore more methods.

Scientifically speaking, telepathy does not exist but this method was working for me so I believed in it and I was making full use of it to connect to my soul mate. Whatever was happening was happening for good. It has given me a completely new prospective on, which path to choose, to keep moving towards the goal.

Let's see where this faith will head me to....

CHAPTER
Twelve

The Love Was Blooming

The faith had shifted my focus from what I feel for him to what he feels for me and why? My expression was growing fearless. My worries had gone. I was getting into a fantasy world with creative imagination and thinking of impossibilities getting possible.

IIe was not around but I was not alone at all. We were not communicating but we were communicating. I did not have his ears to listen to me but I had his soul to feel what I was saying. It was not happening but it was happening with me. Was it an illusion or optimism? Both ways I was enjoying even his absent presence.

Communication is so important...three days ago, I was purging and on this day, I was again beaming with happiness and joy. My heart poured out this joy in a way like:-

My Dear Beast,

Lots of love (I dared to send love). I think you need it, because you are not responding. Are you avoiding me to test my patience?

It's ok... there is no place for ego in love. I will still wait. Your brain can stop you from doing things but your soul is free to communicate. I am aware you miss me, I miss you too.

Today I won't say anything but this one, "I have a past. I thought that was love because we were married. I was wrong. You made me feel, what love seems like. I feel novice for this, as it has never happened to me before.

When I think about you, I feel like pouring all my love and affection and charge your soul completely. I feel like tucking myself into the grip of your arms and feel protected. I feel my femininity again. You tranquilize me with your warm eyes. Your presence appeases my aggression. You hypnotize me with your straight look. My heart skips a beat when you smile. My eyes long to see you. My ears yearn to listen to your voice. All these organs force my feet to move towards you, that's why I keep coming to your office and strike conversations on stupid random topics.

The beginning of our story is beautiful, let's see where we are heading to...

Lots of Love...

I was feeling true passion for this love and was finding new ways and means to nurture it. This love had triggered many things inside me and I could hear the awakening of my soul. I feel love is about acceptance. It's the highest form of meditation. Nothing binds you or blinds you like love.

"You can't blame gravity for falling in love".

Albert Einstein

CHAPTER
Thirteen

A Beautiful Dream

Love was binding my emotions stronger to him. He was venturing into my dreams every day. My day began with him and ended at him. I remember this dream so vividly that, I narrated this dream to my love:-.

My dear Cactus,

Lots of Love...

Oh... shocked? Astonished? Where did this 'CACTUS' come from?

I wanted to see you in my dream. I slept well yesterday and I met you in my dream. After exchanging courtesies, you took me to a river bank. A boat was parked there. You pointed at the boat and indicated with your eyes to board the boat. We sailed to a very beautiful island.

You asked me while sailing, **"Did you again hurt yourself with the door of my office?"**

I replied, "No, because I don't go to your office now a days".

But why?

I said, "Because, I don't get to see you in that chair".

I asked you, "Do you miss me?"

*You replied, "**NO**". (How bad of you... you didn't forget your favorite word even in the dream)*

*There was silence... I could feel the calmness of that place. We both were equally calm. After sometime, you took out a cactus Plant from somewhere and said, "**I want you to be like this..** (What?... like a cactus?)...**The evergreen**". We both smiled. Your sense of humor is as sophisticated as you are.*

*I can't tell you what you did later... you gave me a hard time. You made me listen to **THE HARD ROCK** (my ears are still paining). How unromantic? Isolated Island, beautiful companion, no disturbance amidst the nature.... who listens to Hard Rock?....**The cactus does**...*

'Enjoying it from the side lines'... is no answer to the question "How are you?" Say something... it's difficult to love someone for no response. At some point in life we all need a shoulder to lean on and a hand to hold tight.

* Good Night... *

That day, I had got a meaningful name for him. The name was actually very apt to his personality. Though it's metaphoric but at time these sign and symbols synchronize so much with us.

Cactus is a prickly and pleasing succulent inside; nattily outside. It adapts perfectly to almost any environment. It has patience and it enjoy solitude. It is tough yet gentle. My love was so much like '**The Cactus**'.

But, why he has to love solitude and grow in the

wilderness desert of baking sun? He was actually living a life of solitude. I had hardly seen him enjoying with his group of friends. He would even enjoy his weekends in solitude in a famous local pub sipping his pint of beer alone.

A beautiful dream had grooved me through a comparison to his personality trait. Here it comes again. He was not there around, whom shall I ask? I had no other way but to wait for him.

Human emotions are so complicated. I had just got relieved of my fear of losing him, I had just learnt to leave it to my fate and yet another worry was waiting. This was a caress of care for him.

It was so compelling to think about him all the time, maybe there something so powerful about this love experience; may be the feelings are innocent and pure; maybe we tend to get more sensitive and emotional as we age!!!

Whatever was keeping It alive, one thing was for sure, no one would ever have, had noticed him or observed him and analyzed with an eye of love, the way I did.

The only thing truly unique about my story so far is, the love is still unexpressed, the response is still awaited, the reciprocation was yet far, the uncertainty was eminent, the probability of acceptance and rejection was equally true. But the love was still blooming, the emotion was carefree and the environment was conducive.

Beautiful dream, brought in a beautiful analogy between love and existence. There was more awaiting on the way ahead....

CHAPTER

Fourteen

The Telepathy

There is definitely telepathy between the hearts. Why am I talking about Telepathy here? It was subsidiary method to communicate with my love.

I took help of literature and Google on how to develop telepathy? While learning this new art, I realised, I already knew a part of it and was unknowingly using it in my prayers. I actually had the ability of telepathic communication and telepathic perception, all I needed to do was to polish it a little, to make it more effective.

I relentlessly got onto the job…let's learn a new skill. If I go by logic, science denies the existence of telepathy, but no logic works in love so I closed my mind from logic and began to experiment.

It was working well for me. I don't know what was it? The comfort of my heart to believe it or was I really picking up something substantial? Only time will reveal the truth.

I was really getting some inputs and was trying to relate it to his traits, I knew and I found out from his close friends during informal conversation randomly. 80% of telepathic inputs about him were coming out to be true. Well… fair enough.

Here comes another day, when I sat to write again, as to what I had picked up and how I had decoded it, befitting his personality. The contents were a bit disturbing.

The main trait which I had decoded was, "**He works from his mind and does not give an ear to the suggestions of his heart**". If it was really a struggle between his heart and his mind it was unhealthy '**Discounting his wisdom over his knowledge**'.

Mind is the path of least resistance because it says either yes or no which is easier, on the contrary heart will weigh pros and cons, it will consider minutest of details of matter and try to find a path which is beneficial for all, but difficult to follow at times. It is easy to make up our mind but difficult to convince our heart.

If a heart is open, the windows to vision and to be visionary are open. If only mind is working a person gets restricted to ideas. He was restricting his growth. In a way by choosing the path of least resistance he was choosing to be averse to feelings completely.

Oh my God... what is he doing?

I need to melt his heart, let me caution him...

Dear stone man,

Lots of hammers of love...

See, I am trying everything to melt your heart.

"My heart knows; that your heart know;

it beats for him. Your heart knows the secret of your soul, which is beyond the Capability of your mind to justify". (Confusing?? Read again...)

For Once, let your heart be in charge and let your mind relax. For once, break the monotony, trust someone who loves you. For Once, believe yourself for love. For Once, listen to your inner voice. Just once...

Who am I to tell you all this?

No one, I am no one to tell you anything but I am someone who cares for you.

You believe you have family friends, batch mates? We all feel that way but it's a myth. Parents are growing old, they are worried about your future loneliness when they won't be around. Siblings have new family's new responsibilities. You may have a few friends but they too are busy with earning their living, nurturing their families. Batch mates? They are friends only till you are not seen as the competitor. Superiors want output, juniors seek shelter. No one has time for people like us.

You once mentioned about '**Live in Partner**'. I don't know how much you believe in this concept but there is no harm in giving an insight to the emerging concept. I am not debating "**Marriage versus live in relationship**". I am just trying to highlight a few issues.

Live-in lacks basic concept of union of male and female, which is '**commitment**'. This relation may be an arrangement to fulfill sexual needs and financial needs without any emotional ties. Anyone can walk out of this arrangement without giving any reason.

Life is too uncertain. There are many situations which may occur to us, which may be beyond our control. That situation may be at a point in life, where you may need a companion to walk beside you. But the live in partner is not bound to oblige, so he/she walks out, leaving you abandoned to fend for your own self. Is it worth to invest your time and effort in such a baseless arrangement?

I have an example to quote here. One of my friends in corporate was happy in such an arrangement for almost 3 years. He did not put and ear to his parents wish, neither did he realise his social and moral responsibilities. The life was all about five days of work and a cozy weekend.

One fine day he felt uncomfortable and went to see a doctor. He was detected with kidney infection. One of his kidneys had stopped functioning and the infection was spreading. One kidney was to be removed. The condition was contained, he recouped in six months, **but where was his live in partner?** She had left him, the moment he was detected with kidney infection, because he would not be earning for a few months.

He was left on the mercy of god. Old parents had to come up for help. The guilt which had now overshadowed my friend was manifolds. Guilty for being irresponsible, guilty for not listening to parents, guilty for shirking away from commitment, guilty for being socially irresponsible and guilty for troubling the parents in their ailing old age.

It was very humiliating when he saw that girl, with his own colleague, after his recovery. They both had moved in together.

All I meant to say was, please open your heart for true love. You are head strong, but there is no point in wasting your time to prove something to someone who does not matter. That someone.... 'Remember that some' has moved on. There are people other than that someone who care for you. You should look after them, you should look after yourself.

Who are you? A professional?

No, that is just your identity.

A wealthy man?

No that's a momentary gain.

A healthy man?

No, health is your need for safe future of your kind of life.

A man capable enough to fulfill his needs and wishes?

No that's the way to keep yourself occupied or I would say distracted.

What else?

Whatever else you do for yourself may be good not the best.

It is something like water in the artificial

waterfall, kept as decoration inside the house. Same water keeps flowing and repeating the cycle within the pipes and holes made for its passage. It stagnates and becomes dirty and at the end it has to be changed. You are doing the same thing with yourself. Why do you flow inwards? Why not outwards? Why are you afraid of flowing? Why are you choosing stagnation?

After a betrayal and revival from a bad phase, I have learnt to live again. I have learnt to trust myself and venture into unknown territory without fear. I am sure about existence of problems in life and am equally sure that I will figure out something and some way out.

Now you will ask why to venture at such places?

I will answer the question... **after having such happening life, I feel bored during lull periods, so either something comes to me or I bang into one.**

I accept life the way it comes to me. I don't try to riggle out of it to my comfort zone. That enables me to put requirements of others in my priority list and responsibilities towards them before my own very self. Happiness on my face is the reflection of my contentment. I am not saying I am the best, I just mean this can also be one prospective of life.

Now you will ask me, why am I preaching?

I know you are irritated and angry at me.... you must... I have spoken about so many things without knowing you... without listening to you.... how dare I?

But I have not judged you. I am saying all this because...(you know it)... and I can't see you decaying within. Eyes are mirror of human heart. I have read your eyes and have felt your soul as mine, I have heard your heartbeat as mine, I have absorbed your feelings as my own.

Somehow today I felt you are with someone, who does not have good feelings for you, who is using you for his/ her benefits. You are not receptive and I am draining out of energy.

Take care....be safe for me...

The telepathy was working. It told me as much without a conversation. I am excited and am ready to know more.

CHAPTER
Fifteen

Another Level Of Love

Time had caught up pace, so did my awakening. The telepathy had revealed the enigma to quite some extent. My mind was de cluttering and visions were getting clearer. I had read it in a book, "Love is the ultimate meditation" now I was experiencing it.

One afternoon, I saw such clear vision about a very abstract experience which thrilled me completely. It was as if my soul was poking me to find out more. There was more to it. This was not a coincidence it was well planned; what was it about?

I lived up to my resolves and picked up 'Mr Parker'. Only 'Mr Parker' can dig it deep and assist me in my research. Mr Parker and I were hell bent to decode the vision and we researched till we got satisfactory answer.

All possible means were explored which included my spiritual teacher, online legends and my conscious to authenticate the version with logic. 'I like to learn and decode things my way'.

I just wanted to share my research on that with my love because it was a very beautiful interpretation of the bond between both of us and the reason of that bond was beyond imagination. I was really excited. I could not resist writing down this thrilling and unique revelation.

My Dear Cactus

Lots of pruning of your Thorns with lots of love...

Today after an official chat when I asked you, "Can I ask you something other than professional topic"? You said, "Permission denied".

Well... ok... you can deny permission to text but you can't say don't write...

Your Denial for a conversation pushed me to a new level of understanding.

The Revelations of telepathy have turned the tables, now nothing is about me, everything is about you. I was still happy... I got back from work and by the time my domestic help got me lemonade, I closed my eyes and relaxed. I was contemplating, why did you say permission denied? I think you were aware as to what I would have said so, your soul sent me **I love you** in the form of **"Permission denied"**. The contemplation was still in progress that I got a very Vivid flash.

I saw, we both were sleeping in remote areas miles away from each other. A bright Orange flame rose from your body and red flame from mine. The flames rose up in the sky and swiftly moved towards each other and merged, Spreading Rainbow like colors everywhere".

The lemonade was ready. While sipping the drink, I recollected the vision. I was inquisitive to know about it. I gave a call to my spiritual teacher, she took a while and said, "Two Flames could be twin flames". She touched upon the topic and explained the basic concept. But I needed to know more, so I switched on the laptop and began.

I have come to know there are signs and indications when you meet your twin, then there are stages of development. I will tell you the symptoms first:-

Remembering always.... my day begins with you and ends at you.

Chakra activation... I don't know much about chakras but I think to fall in love with you is result of activation of my heart Chakru.

Seeing In To Soul... I peep into your soul through my heart and through your eyes.

Fated Meeting... meeting is definitely fated. Universe conspired my sudden shifting to this place.

Experiences.... I have undergone pain in my past, you must also have gone through some painful patch, generally during the same time. We can find out while talking in person.

Both Seek Each Other... that's why I could leave the baggage of past and bad Karma and reached you as a pure soul. I am sure so did you.

Share a Secret World ... I have gained the confidence to drop my Guard in front of you, in spite of very less personal introduction. I think that's what secret world of comfort refer to.

Telepathy.... *the most suited and justified symptom. Telepathy between us is very strong. I can see through you telepathically.*

Dreams and Astral Encounters.... *I had two premonitions about you, today was third one. These are Astral encounters, it only happens for people accepted by soul.*

Eternal Awareness.... *I am feeling awakened to love, compassion and many things. This growing love has engulfed me.*

The concept says universe is a combination of Yin and Yang, Nar and Nari, Positive and Negative, so is our soul twin energies... Feminine and Masculine. Both energies incarnate, reincarnate and continue their journey separately Learning, awakening, growth, knowledge and Karma. The aim of burning of flames in so many karmic cycles is to merge into Master Soul. These Flames are meant for Union before achieving their ultimate aim.

These twin flames cross path in many births but can't unite till they achieve same frequency or same Karma. The fast learning and awakening soul becomes Chaser and slower flame becomes Runner. In our situation it is obvious who is a runners and who the Chaser is. I know you are enjoying attention of the Chaser. Please grow up fast. Please don't take time till 65 years of age.

I enjoy giving you attention and love the way you smile after bugging me as a reward of winning over the attention.

Lots of love..

Till now I could categorize people around me as friends, acquaintances, and soul mates; today I have realised these three categories cover everybody except one who is a Twin Flame.

What is love?

Is it an emotion, feeling, passion, addiction, devotion, attachment, belief, care, concern, pain, tears, all of them or none?

It's the most mysterious word I have learnt in my life, it's inexplicable. Most of us remain confused between love and lust. If love is lust then what is a mother's love to a child? What binds humans to nature? What binds us to our pets? What binds us to God? Isn't it strange?

I was so in love with love that I started looking inwards to dig out the answer; love just happens... it's not penurious of any trigger or incident or requirement... it just happens.

Does love exist in us or we exist in love?

It was pretty intense. Love, to my wisdom is all about empathy and compassion and both the terms are not just feelings they are practices, a part of one's characters, which exist in a soul connected to its source. Love has many levels, it is manifold.

Literature explain five types of love, the essence of all types varies in many ways but one thing which is common in all is '*the awareness and recognition of love*'.

Difference between us is due to our different personalities, emotional state and level of awareness but ultimate aim of all for us is to **be loved**. To get love one has to learn love. We are different but same. Love brings us all on a common plane of existence.

"When we are in love, we seem to ourselves, quite different from what we were before".

'Blaise Pascal'

CHAPTER
Sixteen

Love And Responsibility

Life doesn't stop. Everything in our life move parallel. Love definitely has more levels, not only levels but types too. Other types are not consonant with the romantic love but are more stable, fulfilling, healing and readily available. I am talking very specifically about love between parents and children..

Last five months of my life had changed my perception and resolve completely. In last 5 months my life had been full of events. I relocated due to my job, I was dealing with my spiritual awakening, I had my hands full at work and most important and painful was my father was detected with cancer. The test of heart surgery, coincidently led the doctor to identify this problem which was breeding in the body of my father for years.

I had not even overcome the overflow of responsibility cladded emotion to look after my father that my cup of love was suddenly filled with another type of love. To be specific, I was now floating between *The Storge*; love between parents and children and *The Agape*; the Universal love for *My Dear Cactus*.

He was not there and I had to move on leave for chemotherapy of my father. I was going to be out for a week. Till about a month and a half ago, I had no worries about anything, the aim to fulfill the duties towards my parents was clear to me.

That day, while packing my luggage, I was wondering how the life has taken a sudden turn that Mr Parker and my paper pack are also accompanying me in this short travel. The feeling of **may not be able to write** any letter to my love for seven days was really sinking.

I sat down to write down my emotion of that moment to my love:

My dear attention seeker,

*Today I went to one of your favorite eating joints. '**Someone was tired once because his age is catching up to join the gang that day**'. You were right, you are about to be 40...old age is really catching up.*

I may not be able to write to you for next seven days, as I am going for the treatment of my father. Papa is getting admitted for his chemotherapy. I really hope he recovers fast and responds to the treatment. It is still easier to tolerate pain on your body but it's unbearable to see your loved ones in pain. God give me strength to bear that.

Do you realise, how much do I love you? I know you know that. I have already started missing the precious time of my day when I connect with you and write these words on your heart and your heart response to me.

Seven days without this communication in that kind of turbulent scenario is a very tough call for me. You know?? No one in the family knows that papa has such a serious ailment. So far even my mother is unaware. It's going to be difficult to keep it hidden before first therapy at least, which is the most crucial one, let's see.

I never found myself in this kind of helplessness except on the day I had signed my divorce decree. Somewhere deep inside my soul, I feel we are meet to be together. **Now don't take me as a project to prove me wrong.** *Listen to your heart and tell your mind to shut up.*

Do you realise one thing? I don't know anything about you and I don't even feel the need of that either. I love everything related to you. Your name, your silence, your smile, your anger (I can read it in your eyes). I can listen to your silence, I can feel your restlessness, and I also know that you intentionally make a phone call then we travel to office in same cab in order to avoid me.

I sense the maelstrom in your heart when you find yourself off guard. I feel love even in your 'permission denied'. I can feel the care you have for me when I am unwell. I sensed...your heart blushed when I said, "you are looking handsome (after the haircut)". I sensed that racing heartbeat, when we were about to collide with each other in the office (but files came in between).

That eye of yours killed me...I notice minutest of detail about you. There is something which always pulls me toward you. I will always love you the way you are.

Imagine... without knowing you, I have this much to offer, the day I would know you, how much more I will have for you? Love never dies, it only increases and truth give strength to this feeling. Will you listen to me once? Be true to yourself, listen to your soul, believe in God, have faith in love, try and trust me, I won't fail you... because (you know the reason)

Drive safely

That night, before sleeping I was comparing the scenarios. Everything in life goes parallel. We cannot put one thing on the hold while dealing with the other. When I was dealing with responsibilities, Love Came my way... and when I was yet planning to give attention to this long awaited love and was wrapping myself into this feeling…here came the call of responsibility.

That night, I realised how important it is to compartmentalize our hearts. Switching from one compartment to the other makes life so much easier.

In that situation, I really wished I was Aladdin. I would have reached Cactus, hugged him tight and would have soothed my soul.

It was really strange for me to see my own self juggling between love and responsibility and trying to maintain the balance between both because both were equally important for me.

Life is a journey it never ends, it just takes many twists and turns on its way and keeps going...

CHAPTER
Seventeen

The Complex Human Emotions

Once you start loving someone, it is hard to stop. Even a busy day full of running around, mental rigmarole, exhausting routine and mind draining effort to maintain the composer (as an eldest child of the parents) could not obstruct the connection between my love and me..

Between one task and another, I got windows to think about my love. Those intense human emotions were ruling my life at that moment.

I think emotions are intertwined. One emotion can support the other in a constructive way or a destructive manner, depending upon one's perception. In my case the emotion of love had grounded me and stabilized me in a way that I was able to manage the other emotion of responsibility fairly well.

I found myself more accommodating for feelings, softer than before in my dealings and more confident to face that situation at family front. I wanted to express this change to my love and wanted to share the events of last 18 hours which were not communicated, so I took out my letter pad.

My Dear Cactus,

Yesterday I was travelling and today I was busy at hospital. I have just returned, had dinner and sat down to write this letter. I have missed you every minute in the last 48 hours. I felt as if the part of my life has gone missing. Wherever I go, the compass of my heart still points at you.

I am here for my father, I am looking after him and things out here and still a big part of my mind revolves around you all the time. I am completely in love with you. How so ever busy I am, I check my WhatsApp many times in a day. I keep looking for some response from your end on my not so important text.

By not responding, you are putting me through an extremely difficult test during very difficult times and situations.

I am one woman who does not give anything more than '**the due**' to anyone. If you were any other man, I would have felt bad and under the influence of the woman inside me, I would have just chucked him off my life, but you are my love and there is no place for ego where love exists.

Yesterday a very cute little boy travelled with his mother on next berth to mine in train. He kept on looking at me from his mother's lap, till I pick him up and played with him.

He had very beautiful, innocent, big, sparkling eyes like yours. Very cute, little, sharp nose like yours, beautifully carved lips with cute smile like yours, thin and long fingers like yours and round face with arched eyebrows like yours.

While playing with the cute little monster, I thought, you must be like him during your childhood. I don't know why I see you everywhere... I might sound stupid but it's true.

When will you open up? I hope by now you have realised that you mean something to me and the word is 'the world'. I really hope you know how much I love you and also wish that you live these memories while reading them. I have never felt as connected to a man ever before.

I have my soulmates and I connect with them the way soul mates are supposed to but with you feeling and intensity is different. I will tell you about them in person.

I want to speak a lot but all have slept and I need to switch off the light. See you in my dreams... Miss you a lot...

Good Night...

The emotions were overwhelming. The response of a person to a situation is somewhere related to either of the two emotions; **love or fear.** In my case I was going through both of them together. Love for my love and fear of losing my father. One feeling made me skip my heartbeat every time it crossed my memory lane and the other feeling sunken my heart.

When I look back, that time was really testing time for me. There was uncertainty in love there was uncertainty in fear, there was no emotional support of my friends and family because no one knew anything, there was pain behind the façade to pose strong, there was doubt in the prayers.

Everything was helter-skelter nothing was in place. I wonder how much was the strength of that love? He was not there still he was there, he did not exist as my lover still he existed, he did not express anything still I felt as light as feather, he did not even know any of my emotions as yet, still I felt his presence. Without doing anything sane he had his throne in my heart.

Would you call it love...or chemical imbalance of mind due to complex human emotions?

CHAPTER
Eighteen

The Dilemma

Uncommon things are bound to happen with common people while managing mundane issues of life. These mundane issues may overpower us, when they come all together, as a big crisis against time and resources.

Managing relationship, coping with pain, managing the composure, fighting low energy levels, keeping things together and managing overwhelming one-sided love with no response from the other end are a few to quote.

Here comes another such day during the treatment of my father. I was not worked up, I knew what's my course of action at hospital, and how am I supposed to manage worries to encourage my parents at the same time.

But… all of a sudden out of nowhere a small issue came up, although it was small but that was not the right time for it to happen. My emotions were at the brim and I was not ready for it.

That situation came and went, I had no time and place to pacify myself at the hospital, so I waited to come back home. My only let out was a letter to my love. I just wanted to pour out, so I sat down and scribbled everything in a hustle:

Dear Sir,

Lots of love...

Today I am writing to you with mixed feelings. I have a lot on my platter to deal with. Every uncertain has become more uncertain. Today was a very heavy day for me.

I had prepared myself for anything at my family front, when my father was detected with this, but I think the parent's worries for us had also increased. At this point of life also they are more worried about a marriage proposal for me. They are looking for a little ray of hope related to my alliance.

Today I am in a catch twenty two situation. I was running for blood and injections for the procedure of my father. To my horror, I bumped into a man in the corridor who is one of the prospective proposals. I had been avoiding a conversation or a meeting with him for obvious reasons. As usual god made me face my fears. He walked with me to my father's ward. I went numb and was completely in trance as we walked down the corridor. He was talking to me and I was completely absent minded. Although, he gave me the benefit of doubt of being preoccupied but heart to heart, I was absent from that situation and that spot.

My father had a ray of hope, but I can't give him the false hopes. Most important for me was to speak to that man and put the matter aside. I could not do that because he left in hustle.

Later on, I spoke to my mother and told her

that 'I am in love with you'. I also told her that it's my side of story and I don't know how you feel about me. She just heard me, did not give any response, she has more important matters at hand as of now I guess!

My dilemma is whether to talk to the man who is ready or to wait for the one who is not aware? I have got the love of my life, I just don't want to lose it at any cost. Please listen to your heart and mine. The whole universe is echoing "she loves you... She loves you..."

Listen to your heart just once.

Lots of love...

That day, I was given a little shake up by the universe. Since last so many days, I was living like nothing else exists around me except **him** but ***where was he?***

I was absolutely sure about one thing that he may get a woman who is not with a tag like me and maybe much younger than me; but no one can care about him the way I do.

I didn't want to force myself upon him but at the same time, I was not even ready for another refusal. I didn't want to stand in front of mirror as a loser... I am not that bad...I don't deserve a heart break again". I did not know what's there in the folds of future at that time, "***He Was My Present***".

At that time, was I struggling with that small situation, which probably would have faded with time or was it a reality check of my one sided love by my dear universe?

It was a point to ponder upon. Amidst so many matters, love for Cactus also popped up like a pimple on the prom night, because it gave me a feeling of un-fulfilment for the first time. His silence was not just.

> **Me: *I am pretty happy with life...***
> **Life: *OK...let me see...***

CHAPTER
Nineteen

Pain To Power

I believe every day brings a new hope. The dilemma had been conquered by the strength of love.

I believe we go through dilemma only when, we allow ourselves to believe that only two option exist in a situation and we have to choose one, however in reality both the options may not be acceptable options. There is always a third option to deal with a situation in a better way.

I had chosen that third option and I was happy about it. I took a right decision at right time. I was now more convinced that conversation is always a key to resolve matters over contemplation. What lead me to that action was again at a point of decision, '*to be strongest at the weakest point of conviction*'.

I was shaky at the thought, "*Will he love me back?*" I still took a leap of faith and jumped off the cliff.

To be with him was a dream, to get to his heart was a desire and to put other things on hold, to travel from my dreams to my desire was the challenge.

So I gathered courage, accepted challenge and got to work. Result was excellent. It's so true, "*Being deeply loved gives you strength, loving someone deeply gives you courage*".

I wanted to protect my love, so I did it. I could not wait for the day to pass. In the night I sat for my favorite work:

My Dear Monster,

Lots of Love Filled Punches...

After two days of turmoil, I am much at peace. I have told two things to my mother with full confidence. Firstly that, papa will be fine because he has responded well to the treatment. Secondly that "I love Cactus". So, as of now other proposals has been put on hold.

Imagine the strength of love, I cannot leave the opportunity to be with the other half of mine. I know that you don't want to get married but I don't know the reason. There can be a few possibilities for any man who is not ready to marry. There is no ambiguity in the fact that marriage is a traditional ritual for two people to unite and carry on the traditional values (I don't consider it bad).

What's the need to get married?

*Marriage is the beginning of a lifelong commitment and a new family. Marriage is spiritual and emotional union more than just a physical union. Union is bond like no other, it is to move through the life challenges together. The requirement to be together, is to complete our duty as a human to contribute to the evolution of life. We are happy to be single **but life is to be lived as two...with someone who loves you.***

A woman by nature is a nurturer and man is

a provider. If any of them is not ready to get into their basic nature by avoiding union, it may have many reasons. The major reason is commitment phobia. What leads to commitment phobia is fear. Fear of deep emotional attachment, fear of losing freedom, fear of taking on responsibilities, fear of losing financial freedom, control issues, unhealthy sexual patterns, medical disorder and many more.

I think in our case it is fear of losing freedom and lack of emotional bonding, your take on traditions and maybe a medical disorder (pun intended).

Too much of insight on the topic??? I am such a big chatterbox, *but understand all these talks are to hide my internal consternation.*

whenever I enter into your office the things start falling or I hit my hand on the door or the furniture in your office... All are signs of internal storm.

*So far, all good memories with you are official memories. How strange it is to begin a love story with official memories. It's unique and uncommon. Two shy people **(I know you are smiling... What do you mean? Am I not shy???).** Same office (can't even avoid each other), so many catalyst around, so many opportunities to communicate, handsome man, a pretty woman, what else is required for a tale of love??*

Look at me...why do you think, I write these letters to you every night?

It's because, I feel like investing my time and energy because you have become my priority.

I love you as my right. I want to shoulder your responsibilities. I want to pamper you and to be pampered by you. Yes, I am battle-hardened but I have a softer core.

All I need is emotional support from you. I will be a chirpy partner who will never let you feel alone and will fill your life with happiness. I won't be a liability. A world of our own with everyone along with us. I will never let you down in front of your family and friends.

We both are mature people, already towards the trough of the sine curve of our age, left with a few more youthful years, let's invest them in each other.

As we grow older, the crowd around us will start vanishing due to work, professional competitions, family vengeance, envy, jealousy, unhealthy competitions or life cycle. We are used to certain type of people around us, they leave a very big void at times and at places where there is no look back, not even an option to choose a new path.

I am not best, not perfect, not right maybe, but I am knocking the door of your heart at right time. Open it once, believe me you won't be disappointed. Trust your destiny once. I know you are calm types, bookworm, coffee person, Hard Rock types, loner... (With many boring habits in you). But I will manage.

I am not a bad girl...

Try this opportunity of love...

Lots of Love

That day I had opened my heart towards new opportunities and newer matters of life. May be for the first time, I had dared to touch upon this topic. That was my first step to travel the distance between dream and reality. Now I was on the mercy of hope that he may read it and understand it one day.

It was hardly fourteen days that he had left and my bond with him was strengthening with every passing day. The irony was that the man was not even aware of the budding feelings of love in my heart, sitting miles away from him.

Maybe absence deepens love. If love was simple and easy to get; we would not have been listening to eternal love stories today. History is full of examples...

"If it's simple it's not love".
I was waiting for what is this feeling in my heart
and what is its fate?

CHAPTER
Twenty

The Red Flags

I was a woman, who had recently discovered love in her life. She was happy, beaming, smiling and coping her fears, ready to take a leap of faith, jump into the unknown territory and venture there fearlessly. All this was happening when the love was still unexpressed and one sided.

I was in love with a man who was almost five years older to me. **Was he actually not aware that I loved him?** *Was he acting pricey? Was he enjoying attention? Was he even worth this love? Was my love so pure that I could only see well in him? Was I granting him too much of discount on his rude behavior towards me? Was I ignoring the red flags?*

At times, I felt I didn't want to know him anymore because he always made me feel bad about myself. Whenever I tried to strike a conversation, my confidence sunk into my ankles. He tried his best to avoid me, using every possible method and at the same time he ensured that I know, he has all the time for everyone else but me.

I got angry on him because I was feeling hurt, but I believe there was a stronger emotion than anger and ego which was increasing my threshold towards his rudeness.

Whatever, I was picking up in the form of vibes at that moment from him, was not right. There was something hidden, something unrevealed, something buried deep inside of him. I had started feeling his vexation. We hardly knew each other still we knew so much.

At that juncture, my love was turning more towards care and concern for him. I did not realise, when I stopped thinking about our future together and started to care for his emotions and insecurities (which he had not shared with me so far).

I knew, I may not get this love back from him with the same intensity as I wish to give but I cared the least about that. I did not realise his happiness and joy became more important to me then my own. I didn't know why I was feeling that he needs me, at the same time I was extremely angry on him for his emotional insensitivities.

He was the reason of pain and he only was the cure, so here came another painkiller through Mr Parker.

My Dear Don,

I am very angry with you...

I am sensible enough not to disturb you when you are off work. I don't call you, I don't even bombarded you with the messages on phone but it's beyond my capacity to bear no communication with you and more unbearable is to see no response.

What's there to hide? Who is checking you accept your own conscious? It's not a crime to be a bit nice with someone who is giving you time and importance. It strengthens my belief that you know what I have for you in my heart and also that you to have feelings for me but you are acting like a player. It may also be true that you love me more than I do to you.

I was contemplating, how to convey my love to you? In last few days I have found out that there is some hitch with you. Either you are shy and are unable to face it or you are phobic and not ready to commit.

*I messaged you today and asked you; have seen the movie **AS GOOD AS IT GETS**. You know why did I ask? Because both of us are in a similar situation...*

*'Carol' wants to hear something but 'Melvin' is too much into his ego to say that. Carol gets angry due to Melvin's insensitivity, still can't help talking to him and gives a call to Melvin late in the night (In the last part of movie). She says, "**I know you are too old to be ready for this but I am old too to ignore it**".*

You are acting pricey. I have been really open enough and have also been as transparent as possible. Love is like a tender sapling, we need to water it with more love for it to grow healthy but you just don't care. Do you realise how difficult it is to walk on the tight rope of uncertainty, without a single word from the other end.

I was so considerate not to blast a dynamite on your head, without an early warning, so I wrote a letter to you and decided to give it to you before you left for a brake. I thought you will read in the train and will have one month time to think. But scenario is something else.... the reward of being good to you is, pain for myself, because maybe you would not even acknowledge this goodness. I am still writing letters and waiting for a reply on my text from you and you don't care at all.

You should not have done this... I am really sad and angry with you.

Good Night

In the beginning of this scenario, I thought ignoring the other person was the biggest **RED FLAG**. But somewhere I was ignoring them, because I was so much into feeling that I intentionally avoided anything against it.

Irrespective of gender, I feel, when a human is experiencing such an emotion, so densely and intensely, he does not feel like letting go of that pleasure at any cost. I was doing precisely the same thing.

How could I treat him like a man, when his actions and words were reflecting '*Little Boy*'? The Red flags were actually increasing my curiosity to know the reason of his behavior... **Why** or I would say **Why Not**?

**'A boy never knows what he has until he loses her...
A man will never lose her'**

CHAPTER

Twenty One

My Solace

How so ever angry I was with him, how so ever bad was my mood but this time with Mr Parker to connect with my love calmed me down always.

I always felt he was listening to me. I have never written anything this long except my exams or an office draft.

My paper conversation was slowly shifting from the word **I love you** to **what's the Hitch with you???** It was now not about, what I wanted from a relation, it was now about what he may be looking in relation.

But why I was not getting a reciprocal vibe from him at all? Why was he radiating doubts? Why was he ignoring? I was not worried about the future of this relation but the root cause of his indifference.

The invisible bond between him and me was not a physical attraction or material expectation, I connected with him on a different plane altogether. I had no other way but to hit and try. It was not a one to one dialogue but definitely was a strong telepathic message to him.

He was a stone man, difficult to melt and too rigid to mold for love, still I could not accept defeat and started describing the goods and bads, pluses and minuses of being together.

Every major event in our life has timelines. Education, job, marriage, having children, education of children are socially identified main event. Even if we keep our personal aspirations as primary and social aspirations as secondary, we may fail drastically because of the timelines in terms of age. So, wise thing to do is time management.

We both had poorly managed our timelines post getting a job, but the difference was; I had realised it and was aspiring to cope and he had not realised it and was not even interested.

By no means, I wish to say that we cannot begin a life, if timelines are not met, all I mean to convey is that we can save the labor and agony to mold ourselves in old age. I am a firm believer that the plan will fail on the first hurdle, still we must have one. We can start a fresh from anywhere, we can grow under any circumstances, provided we triumph. In our case, my love was happy in his status of stagnation. I had not seen one good friend around him so far. I was also aware that his charm may keep people tied to him for some time, but ultimately he will end up aloof.

Triumphant will try, they can fall but are courageous enough to stand up and try again; but somewhere deep inside me, I was afraid that my love may not be able to do it, because he was just not ready to leave the old templates. He was not only being stubborn but was hindering his own growth as a man.

God help those who help themselves but I believe in his case God wanted to poke him through me to wake him up and move ahead.

I didn't know why we were destined to meet and why we

crossed our path here, but I definitely knew that nothing happens without a divine planning.

MY DEAR WISE MAN,

LOTS OF LOVE...

Though I am angry with you, but I still care. In the last 24 hour, all I could think was, "What will make you understand that you are not managing your timelines". You are mature, not at all impulsive but definitely careless and casual. Are you afraid of losing your freedom to a companion? (This was the only hitch I could figure out, after lots of brainstorming).

I feel like sharing something with you. I won't give you the logic of old age because we humans can feel lonely, stressed, depressed, sad or helpless at any age and stage of life. We generally hear that we would need a partner in our old age. It does not mean that we would look for a companion in old age, it means that we will grow old with a person who will be our companion through thick and thin of life.

When we are young, we have money, power, grit and strength to face challenges and undergo stressful rigmarole of life. We can experience love and affection holding each other's hand during most testing times of life.

Let's face it, everyone on this earth lives with one big and one small problem at a time. The scope and intensity of the problems may vary but believe me pain to face it is the same.

When two people, who have dared to commit, grow older with each other, being each other's strength during tough times, contributing positively and negatively in each other's life, keeping a child alive in each other, complimenting each other's flaws, boosting each other during low tides of life..... They evolve.

When they grow old, they have already invested their time and energy in each other. They have common things to discuss, they have common incidents of life to talk about, to remember and feel happy in re-living those moments which they have created for themselves over the years.

They may be uncommon in many ways but they have learnt to respect that uncommonness in each other. They may be different at the end of the day but in a way they are the same because they have developed companionship.

"Companionship is not something which occurs to us in one day; it's developed over the journey of life"

Now coming on to our case...

If you have an accommodating partner, you can always enjoy your space (I have enough of my own to deal with). I will be loving, caring, affectionate and understanding in all aspects. I will not pick up on you for frivolous issues like... why didn't you pick my call? Why are you late? Why did you not take me out for dinner?

You did not give me my favorite flowers on my birthday... you forgot our anniversary etc. That does not mean I won't fight, but reason has to be worth fighting for.

I am self-sufficient financially, I have my own identity and I am no maintenance for you. We can handle all matters pertaining to us, family, friends, extended family etc. I am gullible, ever smiling, optimist, mature yet as a child at heart. I don't need big things to be happy, I can find joy in the smallest things; as small as washing my fountain pen and enjoying the flow of their nib.

Look at the brighter side. Set your beautiful heart free from the clutches of your brain and let it breathe. I had read it somewhere, "A good loyal woman is one of the greatest gifts a man can have in his life, but it takes a man to realise it". God has given us opportunity, listen to the message of the universe. Unlike misfortune the fortune knocks at the door only once, if you don't open it, the Fortune moves to the next door.

Why you?

I never felt such a deep connection with anyone else but why you? In the last eight years I have come across many genuine and not so genuine men. Many fake people, with fake intentions contacted me. A new fraud, a new method and a new lesson every time, made my intention stronger. I avoided meeting anyone and slowly learnt to read the vibes over the phone. So far my intuition has never failed me.

Now a stage has come that I don't have to put efforts to read somebody's vibe, it automatically blinks a warning in my mind. In your case though the warning is 'amber' but the synchronicities have been unique. I have seen rainbows, feathers, flowers, and fragrances in my vision. You are different.

You are not an acquaintance...

You are not a friend...

You are not even a soul mate...

You have been indicated as a twin flame...

Twin Flames in a tough call over other three but I think with you I am ready to take this call.

What about me?

I am not a mystery princess, but there is much more behind my smile. Everyone sees me what I appear to be... except those who know the real me. You also saw what I chose to show you. I see a man in you who would be able to reach my softer feminine side. I am sure you would like to find out more...Let's give it a try... I am not asking you to marry me but there is no harm in knowing each other.

Good Night

I was emotionally low because everything was happening within me. I was transforming. Compassion and consideration had filled my pores.

Though it was painful and suffocating but I knew that transformation happens for good. I had my solace to share my pain and my experience with. I was now at emotional ease.

> *Mr Parker was my solace and my solace was my companion.*

CHAPTER
Twenty Two

The Awakening

Twenty days had gone past that I had heard his voice. All I had was some disjointed pieces of subconsciously collected information and my solace..

We generally relate love with pain, but I wanted to see it in a different light. Love has either made history or has ended up as a beautiful story of **Happy Ever After...** At that juncture I did not know the fate of my love, will it be a "Historical incident" or a story "Happy Ever After" or something else.

I had decided, not to sulk over petty issues, so I found out a new method to avoid pain... That was to see humor in every positive or negative episode here after.

I did not know if this experiment would succeed or not but I still made a pact with myself that, I will give it my best shot. I was not only a lover to my love, I was a daughter to my parents, elder sister to my siblings, part of somebody's team as a professional and above all a living human being who deserves to be happy.

That day, I took out all the letters which I had written till then and the outflow of emotions was just too unique and beautiful. I had reunited with this side of mine after years...

My Dear Love Pot...

Today I took out all the letters I had written to you and read them. I have realised that I am head over heels in love with you.

How much I trust you... I can speak and discuss anything with you. How much I miss you? How much time am I investing in you? How many prayers I chant for you? How much do I wait for you? At the same time, I am the only reason for feeling of anger, disgust and being ignored because I have not yet expressed myself. My situation remind me of a shayari from my college time:

MAIN APNI MOHABBAT KA SHIKVA TUMSE KAISE KARUN

MOHABBAT TO HUMNE KI HAI TUM TO BEKASUR HO.

I caught hold of an old college journal. I was the editor of the Hindi section. There was a page each for the whole publication team. I wish to share with you that one page on me:

"The talented poetess with the gift of gab".

Oh dear... You brighten not only the club, but our hearts with your smile... Keep smiling... Make the world worth living".

I was nostalgic to read this. I met the younger me. This page was published 15 years ago. The younger me was so cute, sweet, adorable, a Pandora of mischief.

I remember I wrote my first poem on my childhood, "Mera Bachpan". Here I recollect a few lines...

MERA BACHPAN JO MUJHE BAHUT AZIZ THA,

MERE HATHON SE NIKAL KAR KAHIN CHHIP GAYA HAI.

CHHIP GAYA HAI WAHAN, JAHAN USE DHUNDHNA MUSHKIL HAI,

PER CHHIPA VOH MERE NAZDEEK HI KAHI HAI...

I had unpolished talent, I had words, I had an imagination, I had expression. I gave it away to live a life with someone who did not value any gesture, any quality, not even my life. In the struggle of survival, I lost myself, I lost my innocence, I lost my comprehension, I lost my vision, somewhere I lost my loved ones, my home and I lost my roots.

KITNA KHAUF HOTA HAI SHAAM KE ANDHERON MEIN

POOCH UN PARINDON SE JINKE GHAR NAHI HOTE.

What an irony???

YEH JINDAGI HAI SAHIB

ULJHENGE NAHI TOH SULJHENGE KESSE?

BIKHRENGE NAHI TOII NIKHRENGE KESSSE?

See the magic of love, I am changing every day, becoming a better version of 'me'. I am forgetting and foregoing my fears and pains. It feels like:-

MOHABBAT MEIN NAHI FARQ JEENE MARNE KA,

USI KO DEKH KAR JEETE HAIN,

JIS KAAFIR PE DAM NIKALTA HAI.

I know shayari may not interest you, but please bear with me just for a change. Imagine my plight, what would not happen to me in years, happened to me instantly.

MAUT KI HIMMAT KAHAN THI HUMSE TAKRANE KI,

KAMBAKHT NE MOHABBAT KO SUPARI DE DALI.

Above all, you see everything, you feel everything, you understand everything but you don't acknowledge.

CHALO MANA KI HAME PYAR KA IZHAAR KARNA NAHI AATA,

JAZBAAT NA SAMAJH SAKO ITNE NADAN TO TUM BHI NAHIN.

Above all; so many days without you. Come back early or do one thing...

ZARA SI FURSAT NIKAL KE KATL HI KAR DALO,

YOU INTEZAR MEIN TADAP KAR MARNA, HAMEN ACHCHA NAHIN LAGTA.

I miss you terribly. Today while doing yoga, I started smiling for no reason; my yoga teacher asked, "What happened?" I didn't have any answer. You don't even realise the depth of the matter.

UNKE SOCHNE SE JO AA JATI HAI MUH PAR RONAK,

WOH SAMAJHTE HAIN BIMAR KA HAL ACHCHA HAI.

I know you are precious, because I love you. I am also not less than a diamond. You would need a magnifying glass to search for a girl nearly like me. So value me...

YE NAMUMKIN HAI KOI MIL JAAYE TUM JAISA,

PAR ITNA AASAN YAH BHI NAHIN,

TUM DHUNDH LO HAM JAISA.

Oh my god... After so many years, back to my college days. I am feeling so rejuvenated, I mean each and every word of this letter, full of immaturity, so much fun yet so true.

Still... Thank you for reading this teenage college type cheesy letter. At times it's good to feel young, especially when someone's age is catching up. Let's know each other... There is a lot like love in life.

Lots lots of love...

Good night...

After enjoying my solace and being back to college life, I slept. I woke up at 3 a.m. in the morning with a very scary vision about my love. It was so real and intense that I could not sleep again and started writing at that hour of night.

My dear love...

It's 3:10 a.m. In the morning. I have woken up with a very scary vision. I had once in my mind to write a text to you on mobile but I refrained.

The vision was about your internal turmoil. I woke up quickly, prayed for you and sat down to write this.

I had no dream today except this one. Our energies resonate, that's why we connect telepathically. It may be because of your soul to my soul for help or support.

I saw, you were smiling and waving at the crowd (I am also a part of the crowd). You were moving backwards while waving. As you slowly distance from the crowd your smile vanished (a jolt of fear hit my heart hard). There was a path behind the stage leading to the jungle. You started walking swiftly towards the jungle.

You were restless, disoriented and having haunting thoughts in your mind. I ran behind you in the nape of the shrubs. You could not find a way after reaching a point in the jungle and sat under a tree.

You started shouting, actually you were throwing some questions either to the universe or to yourself. You said, "What am I doing? Am I doing the right things? Am I so useless that people can take me for granted? I had not expected this from people I trusted. It might be normal for them, but I am feeling cheated and humiliated and backstabbed".

You were flooded with the thoughts of betrayal and solitude and were groaning in pain. It was beyond me to see you in that pain. I could not stop myself.

The only way to console you at that point was to pray. So I prayed to god to show me the path to your heart, where the cause of the pain is hidden. I concentrated and prayed very intensely in dream, to reach out to the root cause of the matter.

Three words echoed in my mind... "Betrayed", "Manic" and "Transformation". I woke up with a whisper in my ear... The whisper was "The Hermit".

I woke up... What Hermit? What's Manic?

As per dictionary 'Manic' means 'Anxious' (Worried or nervous). As per definition as given on google, "Manic is a subject that plainly demonstrates his liberation, from the object, which causes suffering." That means you achieve instant indifference towards people who have hurt you. But as per another explanation it is a disorder in which a person does not forget and gets into vengeance mode.

Now that makes sense...

What's hermit?

A person living in solitude as a religious discipline. The hermit is also a card in tarot. So I researched more on it. The Hermit is a lone wolf, who spends time in solitude for soul searching and introspection. People are drawn to them for advice.

They have a deep soulful relation with someone, who is a friend first. They feel no one can really understand them so they keep most of themselves to themselves. They choose to live in solitude. They prefer friendship to romantic relationships. They keep their feelings hidden in their head. They don't like rocking the boat in personal relationships because they don't want to feel vulnerable. They connect to their inner light through reading, writing and mentoring. They have heightened sensitivity. They are meticulous and over critical of themselves; fixated on unnecessary details, rather than seeing the clear picture.

The real love is the highest desire of their soul because of the eventful past of failed relationships. Failed relationships were there teachers, who brought them where they are today. To my understanding the connection of Manic, Hermit, Betrayed and Transformation maybe:-

You possess the qualities of hermit, may be due to your temporary or permanent love relations, who betrayed you fully for partly. But you have a manic mind set i.e. "Liberating from the object which caused you suffering". Which means the betrayal was brutal.

Transformation is a state which you may be going through right now. It is like the process of leaving your old skin and generating a new one. This process is emotionally painful because leaving old skin means to fight your own belief system, the deep rooted feelings which are very dear to you.

It is like tearing off a layer of your heart to remove old cladding to make a way for fresh energy to flow in. Regrowth of new skin will be as fast as you have a self realisation through your heart, mind (not brain) and soul.

My love, you already have the inner strength to bear the pain. The only thing you need to keep in mind is to choose the right path towards the transformation.

At this stage the angelic and demonic side of yours will try to pull you towards their path. Listen to the white side of your soul, please don't sell yourself to the devil.

I care for you. I won't say I am worried, because I believe in your strength and wisdom. You will sail through and come out transformed as a beautiful human being.

May god be with us...

I don't take my dreams as dreams only, because in the past I have seen dreams which turned out to be true in later time frames. That dream set me thinking...I tried to reconnect all disjointed telepathic conversation with my love. I opened my notes and went through them. I checked my daily practice journal.

Oh my god... You are really around me. He is actually a hermit. He does not mix around much. He enjoys his Saturday evening in a pub in solitude. He does not have many friends. He is afraid of opening up. He is very meticulous and selective with his words.

People come to him for advice. He is overcritical of himself because I had noticed, he always has set unhealthy challenges for himself.

Most important revelation was that secrecy, which I was feeling with his attitude. Some deep rooted or inexplicable pain. It could be a betrayal or miss understanding.

I always believe, no one is born as an emotionally insensitive person, circumstances make them so. Maybe he had some past, which he has never revealed to anyone because he has lost trust.

That night, I thanked god for being with me in my transformation. It was not only an indication of his awakening but was a very prominent milestone of my awakening as well.

I decided to listen to the white side of my soul and be a good apprentice, who is ready to learn and undergo shedding of old skin and regenerate a new skin completely transformed and at the same time to support my love in his awakening.

While I was writing this chapter, I realised the dream had appeared in my sleep one year ago. I also realised how true it was. I could have taken this as a RED FLAG and would have stopped loving him but I did not, because I cared for him.

That night I thanked god for being with me in my transformation. It was not only an indication of his awakening but was a milestone of my awakening as well.

I decided to listen to the white side of my soul and be a good apprentice, who is ready to learn and undergo shedding of old skin and come into a new skin completely transformed. At the same time to support my love in his awakening.

MAY BE THIS IS CALLED UNCONDITIONAL LOVE...

CHAPTER

Twenty Three

The Curiosity

What was it that I saw that night? I felt as if I am living through that event. While I was narrating the whole scene in the letter I remembered each and every detail. I had been seeing dreams in the past as well, but this time i wanted to find out "why?"

What connects me to the man who is unaware of my feelings for him? How do I see things related to him? What makes me see hints of the future? How do I remember the minutest of details of dreams? These questions set me to explore the possibilities. More so because now the emotions were love predominant.

The first term I encountered was "The Brain Waves". Any process that changes your perception changes your brain wave. The brainwave patterns are related to our circumstances and emotional state. There were many types of brain waves described in various conditions, which synchronized the most with my question was "Theta Wave".

"Theta Wave" occur during sleep or meditation. This is our gateway to learning, memory and intuition. These waves disconnect us from the external world and connect us to the signal originating from within that is self-consciousness. In this state, we see vivid imagery, intuition and information much beyond are conscious awareness. It occurs during the time we wake up or are drifting to sleep.

There were many more things, which were spoken by many researchers but this much was of relevance to my situation. Dreams are difficult to remember, but how do I remember them vividly? It can be done by training our brain waves using meditation.

So, unknowingly I was meditating and was training my brain waves to be more stable. I have been meditating for two years now. It means a de-cluttered mind was the plot for imbibing heightened sensitivity for the intuition which in turn had grounded me and I was able to see dreams and remember them too. Moreover nowadays my emotional state was all full of my love, so I had been able to see that.

Definitely there was more to it. After many conversations with my friends and discussions with people having similar conditions, I caught hold of a book written by 'Orloff' in 1996. The name of the book was "Second Sight" Orloff has explained the word 'Empath', using the main character of the book, who possesses the qualities of Empath.

Empaths are people who can feel others emotions as their own. This was another piece of information which encouraged me to dig deeper. I get goose pimples, when I see anything overwhelming, for example and accident, a beautiful scene, people in pain, a child crying to go to school, a rape victim, a women victim of domestic violence, when Indian sports teams win or lose. Am I an Empath?

That day, I left the research at that. It increased my curiosity and anxiety both. I was curious to know more because somewhere it had triggered my "Self Discovery" but I was anxious too, because I was afraid to know anything unusual. So I immediately switched to my solace:-

My Dear Love,

A very warm hug

I hope you are feeling better now... You scared me. I could not bear your red face full of sweat and eyes full of tears, the pain in your voice and volcano boiling in your heart. I could feel the heat of those intense and mixed feelings of anguish, sadness and being cheated. I may be wrong in interpretation of that but believe me it was extremely painful to live that moment with you, not because I saw you in pain but because I could not go to you and hug you.

I am counting days, hours, minutes and seconds for your return. Why is this happening to me? Why do I get visions or dreams about you which are not related to any romantic fantasy? Why do I miss you? Why do our souls connect so well? Why am I waiting for you? Why has my life come to a halt suddenly? 'Love' is not the answer to all these questions, there is more to it.

Imagine you are in your late thirties and I am in my early thirties. Our love is upper middle age, it's strange but cute.

I believe in companionship and commitment.

Even after a brutal betrayal, I am open to these emotions. In a commitment we love a person with all his/ her qualities and flaws and never leave their hand under any circumstances. There is no definition of the best couple or a successful marriage. It's about, how best is the understanding to achieve compatibility.

I may not be the best, but I read your silence in a way no one else can do.

You may not be the best for me but you soothe my soul and appease my temperament in a way no one else can do. Trust, respect and love develop the companionship. I trust you blindly, I have respect for you in my eyes and have a heart full of love for you.

TAKE CARE

GOOD NIGHT

While writing this letter I realised; I was actually penning down the emotion I felt while watching that dream. The vision was virtual but the way I felt it in my skin that night was real. I had woken up drenched in sweat in my AC room.

Oh My God... I was awakening to a new side of my own self. I don't know what will come out but now I want to know more.

CHAPTER
Twenty Four
The Answer Lies Within

The curiosity was yet not settled. The debate on the topic of *"Why does the deep connection exist between me and my love and why do I have deep emotions of trust, respect and love for him?"* V/S *"Why is he still silent on this?"* was still unconcluded.

The answers to many questions, lie within us. While the debate was going on, a very old event of the past crossed my memory lane.

I realised that many small events may happen at many places, at different times with us but the impact of these events may be very deep. Many of them may be happy ones, many may be depressing and many must have given us some lessons which may fit into a situation subsequently in our life.

An event which may appear inconsequential or normal in nature might have deep hidden lessons in their occurrence, but the lesson may come into light when we actually need them.

The incident was six years old, so I could recollect only those parts of the episode which were pertinent to my current situation. I debated on it on my paper in my favorite way:

My Dear Love,

I was wondering, will you ever categorize these letters as your "Billet-Doux". Most of them are on serious and intellectual topics which everyone does not discuss liberally in a routine life. Without knowing you and your taste I have been doing this a little too freely. What to do??? I feel you can understand all this.

I believe love is a combination of three things; Passion, Warmth and commitment. Passion is relentless longingness, commitment is about belongingness and warmth is about care which fills our soul. I have all three for you. We may term it as love (if you too have the same feelings for me).

Love is a package in which we get respect, trust, space, understanding, responsibilities and emotions as a bonus.

I feel, we both have grown beyond the immaturity of doubt. We can understand what has been said and we can read what has been left unspoken in each other's eyes. We can connect even among thousands of people around us. We may still fight but the battle will not be on mundane topics like other couples because we may just laugh out the routine mistakes.

A smile of love can resolve toughest of conflicts. I am confident that we will be happy if we are together. The only hitch is your love for your bachelorhood.

Today I am going to share a very random

episode of 2012. During one of my official trips to Bangalore in 2012, I got a seat next to Mr Nair, a middle-aged well-dressed man. Over our Conversation he introduced himself as a professor of Physics in one of the reputed colleges.

He was going for a guest lecture. I just asked him what the guest lecture was about. I thought he must be going for some topic of Physics, but contrary to my belief, the subject was nowhere related to Physics.

The professor along with his team had carried out a study on 'The Increasing Trend of Bachelorhood'. He explained, why nowadays people are not getting married and prefer to stay single and also its outcome and impact on the society.

It interested me for two reasons, firstly I was just out of the turbulent waters and was still not confident about "What's next?" on the matter of resettlement. Secondly it was astonishing as to why people are getting into this kind of noncommittal mind set.

In a nutshell he explained, "Lives of men and women have changed drastically in terms of economy, Psychology, Physiology, sexuality, individual aspirations and social system." From joint family concept to nuclear family concept, which is slowly drifting to "No family concept".

Earlier men and women found a sense of freedom in marriage because needs were less and the economy did not affect the emotions. Nowadays people prefer material over relationship and needs have increased, so is the greed. The concept of togetherness has been replaced by the individual aspirations and sharing and caring has fallen prey to the self-centric, short-term achievements of selfish goals.

Both the genders are equally responsible. Men didn't realise where to put a stop on suppressing women and women rebounded and retaliated with the same force and now the situation is out of control.

The need of not to get suppressed and have an identity, has become a fear among women which acts as a negative reinforcement to achieve it. Chivalry is fading, loyalty is dying down and commitment is dreaded by this generation. Everything is need-based including physical desires. No one wants to put efforts to build a relationship because everything is available off the shelf including emotions.

Dating sites are getting into Trend. "Feeling lonely?" Hop on to one of them, put your requirements and response will overwhelm you. That does not end only on requirements; you will also have options to select long term or short term companions. A short term means a one night stand. Today India is a young country, in another decade we will be a country of old people.

He Went On And On...

I have written whatever I could recollect from the reminiscences. The last point was really a point to ponder upon. Just a little loud thinking...

Mr Nair said, "Earlier man and woman found a sense of freedom in marriage". "It's so true... I think we can achieve it by our trust in each other. We will not stall the progress of each other and will grow together. Maturity can always cater for the scope of communication, even in grave conflict.

I think, it just needs a little role reversal of our organs to set things right.

How???

THE MIND is an intellectual who works on logic. It's an expert to deal with things like studies, economy, finances, Material Management, objects etc. The heart is an emotional organ, dealing with virtual things like psychology, emotions, feelings, relation, society, opinion etc.

I feel people who avoid marriage or commitment are the ones who keep material, objects, economy and profession etc closer to their heart (but actually these are not the forte of heart). The heart is emotionally coded so it accepts all of these needs openly as it doesn't ask WHY?

These people ask the brain about love and emotions and the brain says, "No logic found" because the brain is logically coded it discards the ideas related to feelings.

Isn't it wrong???

The same is happening with you. Please employ your right organ for the right job. Three pillars of love are Passion, warmth and commitment which *belong to the cardio department of the body and you are referring it to the Nuro department. That's why your treatment is not working well for you...*

Think about it...

That's all for today...

Good night...

The incident brought a smile on my face that day. That was just a random conversation, which took place between two strangers just to pass time in that small journey.

Mr. Nair may not even remember me today, but that small discussion gave me an answer to a situation completely out of pretext on that day. This situation was not even existing that day.

All answers lie within, one just has to be a little observant of the occurrence. If we are ready to observe that the life surprises us every day. It's rightly said, "To acquire knowledge one must study but to acquire wisdom one must observe."

A little effort gave me an answer today. The lesson was, "If this is the case with my love too, I will have to work hard to convince him for slight modifications, as i know he is headstrong and there is definitely one side of his, which is not known to anyone."

ON A LIGHTER NOTE... MY THETA BRAIN WAVES WERE WORKING WELL...

CHAPTER

Twenty Five

Why?

Once during my internal cross-examination I had answered, "I don't know why but I can tell you how I love him?".

If the answer lies within, then the answer to this question must be within me. The question was "***Why I love him***".

Only a thought towards an unknown man (who is completely unaware of the whole scenario of overflowing feelings at my end) could change so much. I came across the Telepathy, the Twin Flame connection, The Brain Waves, The Empath etc. All these very unusual words for any common person including me.

In lay man language, too much of involvement may be termed as obsession, but can my emotion be termed as ***Obsession***?

I had courage to speak my truth and hear his truth too. I had maturity to accept 'NO' gracefully because we cannot demand love. I did not want to be a third party if he was already in love with someone. **It would have been an obsession if I wanted him at any cost.**

In our case, the scenario was different. ***His happiness was more valuable than my desire. So it was definitely not obsession, it was love.*** It can only be love because my heart was ready to undergo the pain of unrequited love for one smile of my love.

With lots of practice over years I had developed the **Art of Detached Attachment**, but this love was dragging me back to attachments and emotional ties.

Why?

As the answer was within, so I peeped inside and what came out as a very strong voice was:-

My dear tricky love,

You really tricked me today,

I came to know you were back from vacation and would come to the office. Believe me time came to a halt. My eyes got restless and I checked your office a 100 times. I sealed all the letters, put them in a file, put the file in the envelope, addressed it and put it in my bag.

I returned to my room by 3:00 p.m., although you said you were not here still I felt you are around, because the gush of blood in my veins can't lie to me. If you wish to remain secret, it's perfectly alright. It's a matter of six more days.

I have mentioned 'my past' in many letters so far, but every time I get emotional and could not conclude the letter properly. There are many episodes which are very scary to be recalled. While living through them, I died many deaths. Whenever, I try to express my love, myself or my sensitive feelings, the horror of those thoughts sealed my lips. It is as if I have eaten my own heart because of the humiliation, destruction and stigmas I had to live through. It's really hard to explain.

At times I encountered situations where I felt as if someone has removed my clothes in public and people are feeling amused instead of feeling sympathetic or ashamed of someone's act of inhumanity. It is a reality that humiliation and pain of someone else amuse people.

Amidst all this action and reaction, my eyes had been looking for a shelter of someone, who can come up to cover me and save me from that humiliation. The feeling of embarrassment was very horrific, that's why I tried many times but diverted the topic, just to save myself from that horrendous emotion to overpower.

Do you know, why am I sharing this with you? Because I feel you have come for my rescue. I feel you have covered me with your love, wrapped it around me and saved me from that inexplicable pain of the past. I feel the warmth of your love is melting the deep rooted pain from the depth of my heart.

I always tell myself that I would cry to a person who is stronger than me...see I have been opening up to you and I am convinced about my conviction, I believe you and I know, you are the Alpha I can cry with.

The pain is oozing out of my eyes like molten wax. I have never been into the protection of strong arms as yours, ever in my life. I have never felt the warmth of love like that. Your chest seems 'Pious Than Thou' where I want to bury my head and sob.

Why... Why you?

You don't deserve a torn, maligned and ruined woman like me... I am sorry.

Oh come on girl... not like this, not to him... cheer up...

I am not seeking sympathy. I am just being truthful to both of us. I don't feel small or ashamed of crying with you, with ugly looking face and crow-like voice. I believe you don't customize me, you like me the way I am, you can tolerate my mistakes and bear my follies, you understand me completely, you sense my anxiety, you can feel my pain, you know my concerns for you, you can smile at the child inside me.

I feel complete with you and want to live this beautiful fantasy at least once in my life, before moving to the next world. I want to bury my head in your chest, lock that moment and be there forever, in the most comforting solace.

I am not old but the journey from hopeless to hope, from nothing to something, from torn apart to rebuilt, from broken to mended, from love to Indifference and from aggression to forgiveness, has made me strong in my conviction and my skin, where I am; what I am today...

Although, I was never mean to anyone but I have been ill-treated to hilt. After spending peak of my youth struggling to keep my dignity intact, which unfortunately in our society, is in the hands of inconsequential people, who may not have the character to give a character certificate to others. I have found you, who is like a breath of fresh air to me.

I often used to cry myself to sleep thinking that he (my ex-husband) was the most precious thing in my life, because the price I paid for him was exorbitant. I paid it with the precious time of my life which will never return, I paid it with my heart, I sold out my sleep, and still the cost was unrecovered.... I am still paying off in many ways because true love is still awaited.

The nightmare which still haunts me is his "Smirk". I wake up Breathless even if I see it in my dream. I feel he is still strangulating me and will push me off the cliff.... there is no end to it.

Why am I pouring out?

Anyways....

Whenever I feel sad, dug down deep into my agony, I listen to this song:-

I see trees of green... Red Roses too...

I see them bloom... for me and you... you.

And I think to myself.... what a wonderful world.

It gives me hope to move on. I think it takes a lot to speak out about the forbidden stuff. I am not sorry or ashamed that I converse with you on this topic.

Thank you for your imaginary bear hug today...

Good Night

While writing this letter of mine, I smudged the paper, the paper was not even visible due to the flooded Eyes. I was sobbing like a small child, I was feeling warm and protected. I really did…

I did not know… Was he even ready for such an outpour of an ugly reality? Does he even have aptitude to put himself into other shoe and respect the struggle? Does he even have the strength to bear the truth? All I knew was that I can trust him.

He made me feel that I don't only exist but I have the right to live too. It was his presence around that encourage me to make myself visible as a woman. He pulled out everything which was hidden inside me and made it useful. He pulled out my pain to create space in my heart for true love. He pulled out the feminine side of mine which made me outshine my own image of "Strike Lassie". He made me bring balance in my action and worries of people's reaction.

All of these he did effortlessly to an extent of managing it without putting and effort to speak a word. His presence around me was enough for everything. Most importantly for making me meet that spirited girl which always resided in the caged heart inside of me.

I was no more scared of the judgment of people and was free of all negative thoughts about myself. I stopped criticizing people and started admiring the smallest things. This was real me.

I love him because he made me visible in my own eyes. He was the reason that I started seeing good in myself. I had rediscovered a new me, a beautiful me and an amazingly soft and sensitive being of love... that's me.

NOTHING BEATS THE FEELING OF BEING IN LOVE AND BEING LOVED...

I WAS HALF WAY THROUGH...

CHAPTER
Twenty Six

As Clear As Bell

Our own tragic times of despair, bring up worries, sorrow, distrust and frustration in uncertain times. The reflection of difficulties in the journey of life brings up resentment, which in turn pulls us back to our shells. This was what had happened to me in the last almost a decade.

It was my fear to face love and worry to get hurt again, which was holding me back in my shell. The presence of **'my love'** around me gave me the confidence to break free. I could hear my heart singing as clear as a bell, I could see my soul crystal clear. The outpour of the past had cleared the agony and negativity from my system. I was feeling renewed, rebooted and was sure of encountering new adventures and relish in a new way.

After sharing the deepest negative feelings of my past and living through the pain one last time, to pull out the dirt with my own hands and clear the space.

I was very content and peaceful. The Peaceful mind was reflecting serenity on my face. I had cleared the mist and was feeling easy now. I was ready to fill the space with love, affection, gratitude and smile.

Only after a complete cycle of destruction, did I understand myself and in the process of recovery, I discovered who I was. After self-discovery the haze got cleared and the fear to love and be loved vanished.

Now, I was feeling liberated and my own self and had set the horses of expression of my heart beat free. I didn't know how peaceful can be the feeling of this expression of un-reined rebellious thoughts was, until... I read this piece of my own letter from the past.

My dear Po..

A Big Bear Hug...

I am sorry for the volcanic expression of yesterday. I have been very boring with you. I don't bring any romance or exciting fantasies in my letters. Always gloomy or serious. I tried to explode in many letters but it happened yesterday. No more emotional outburst.

I missed you an ocean today. Nothing seems more important than waiting for you. I was missing you so much that it became difficult for me to be in my room, so, I pushed off on a long drive. I have just returned and here I am to speak to you.

I wish to go with you on a long drive, just you and me and love in the vehicle. Imagine you are driving and I am staring at you, mesmerized and lost in that moment of being next to you. You would say, "Don't look at me", I would not listen to you at all. You would start smiling and so will I. I will not trouble you thereafter.

Will you fulfill my wish?

"I want to hold your hand, hug your arm tight, put my head on your shoulder, close my eyes and sit for a while without speaking a word.

I want to live each and every moment of life with you... I want to cook for you... I want to hold your hand and walk on the shores of wet sand bare feet... I want to see every sunrise and sunset with you... I want to listen to your voice every day... I want to hug you every day... I want to say 'I love you' every day... I want to share your happiness and own your sadness... I want to be the reason for the smile on your face every day... I want to pray for you every day... I want to see you applying your after shave every morning... I want to move my fingers in your hair... I want to give you a flying kiss while you leave for office every day... I want to have my evening tea/coffee with you every day... I want to be a part of you and your family... I want to share your responsibilities... I want to put on 10 kgs once for you... I want to be with you for rest of my life".

Be my man...

I know 'yes' is a difficult word for you and it's the reverse in my case. We are different but same, let's take a middle path, let's try it once, let's give a chance to each other, let's share and care for each other, this is the right time the right place and right us.

Oh God's heaven... after opening up considerably well, finally I could convey what I wanted to tell you all these days but ended up beating around the bush every time. We are 30 plus and this little effort is not asking too much from ourselves.

It's time to act upon... let's try once.

Good Night

Such a relief it was, finally the wish outshined and came out of my mouth. He definitely is my desire not my need. These are little mercies of God upon us to be able to enjoy small moments of joy in our lives. There was nothing out of the world in this for almighty but definitely I looked my world into it.

After the bumpy ride of self-discovery in the last almost two months of love, I have encountered many happy, sad, thoughtful and curious moments. I underwent change. I understood what I wanted and I realised who I was.

Though the knowledge is never enough, the beginning of this new journey was very thrilling just like a roller coaster ride. I was enjoying it. The sound of my love and my wish was **AS CLEAR AS BELL** in my heart, mind and soul. I was no more in dilemma of...

"SHALL I? Or SHALL I NOT?"

CHAPTER
Twenty Seven
The Waiting Was Over

Finally the day arrived when he was back. We were breathing in the same air again. We were again next door to each other. Nothing had changed but a lot did.

I was not the same woman, he had left behind a month ago. I was free of my past ties and its pain. Although, I had forgiven the reason for those past pains, but in the last one month I had to let go of everything related to my past and create space for 'my love'.

I had created many dots of various experiences...all that was required was his will to join those dots. I was connected with my love in many ways, yet a connection was awaited from his side.

There was a unique feeling of accomplishment in my heart. I was not afraid to face him, yet I was afraid. A lot was happening inside my system. Eyes were eager to see him but were shy, ears were longing to listen to his voice but were beeping, and heart was feeling his presence but was pouncing. I was excited, happy, hesitant and shy...all at the same time.

Generally when I am confused I talk a lot.

Oh...girl... hang on... breathe... relax... smile... gather yourself and go to the office. Oh God.... I wish he would reach the office after me. I will die if I see him there at the gate or at the corridor. I was praying and entering the office with shaking legs and a shivering body. I gained my senses in the evening and wrote whatever had happened during the day.

My dear divine masculine,

Love from divine feminine

I want to share my feelings of that moment with you, when I saw you after one month today.

I was very restless and eager to see you but went numb. I thought of taking a stroll before entering the office in order to stabilize my nerves. The moment I entered office… to the horror of my heart… I saw you just there. I went blank, my legs started shivering and my heart slipped down to my stomach and started beating like bellows. I felt I would collapse in front of you. I went into a trance. I gained myself back with your groovy voice coming from the far end of the tunnel,

"Good Morning Madam"…

"G…G…G…Good morning sir, sorry my mind was somewhere else".

I accompanied you to your office but could not stand there for long.

I was happy to see you back and happier to see your ring finger empty. I felt like crying out loud and telling the birds on my window "My love is back". I wish I had x-ray eyes to see through the walls. People came to my office and went, I don't remember anything. Only one line was echoing in loop in my mind………

"Good Morning Madam."

Then...I saw the packet of the letters in my drawer. After sometime, I went to your office with a few lame points and of course lots of feelings sealed in that packet, but I could not gather the courage to handover the packet to you. The packet came back with me.

It was time to wind up for the day and come back to our rooms, but I had no power and courage to travel back in the same car sitting next to you. So I decided to give it to you and run... and...I did that...

Believe me, I am so anxious for your reaction. I feel like going invisible. Please don't get angry. Please feel my love and live those moments I have captured in my letters. I don't mean harm and don't expect anything except an eye of love.

Oh God give me strength...

Happy Reading...

I was tossing and turning in my bed for the whole night. Every now and then, I heard the sound of his shoes approaching my door. I felt the doorbell was about to ring.

I felt he would ring the doorbell, I would open the door and he would ask me with his arms wide open, **"CONGRATULATE ME"**. I felt, I would sink into his arms and let my heart melt in the warmth of that eternal love. We both will have no words to speak but the silence will say it all. I will not let him go away ever.

I wished time stop there till our souls healed fully. Suddenly the morning alarm sounded. I came out of my beautiful imagination and laughed at myself, **"Silly Girl"**.

The human heart is so gullible, just one small feeling of love can heal all the past injuries.

I did not know what was there in the folds of the future...

That was my D-Day...

I lived for two years in the feeling of love for MY LOVE. It was initial two months only in which many things about me were not the same anymore. The story of two months has been elucidated in "MIRVANA…the story of my defiant love".

Human wisdom comes from life experience. Love is much beyond human wisdom. One lifetime is not enough to take a dive, deep into the ocean of love and gauge its depth.

Love happens when you least expect it…it springs up as if out of nowhere, shakes us up, swirls our thought process, shrugs our system and brings us in alignment with our senses and the higher purpose of life. Being selfless and loving unconditionally are very fascinating terms to use but it squeezes the heck of courage and patience out of a lover.

The wait was not over yet…life took an unexpected turn after MY D-DAY…

I am resting first part of my story here…

I want to know ….will the outcome be predictable to the readers?